GOING DENTAL
in New Jersey

THIS BOOK IS FICTION.
ANY RESEMBLANCE TO PERSONS LIVING OR DEAD IS STRICTLY
COINCI**DENTAL**.

ISBN 10 0615459846
ISBN 13 9780615459844

GOING DENTAL
in New Jersey

A BOOK BY LORI FRAN

A FICTIONAL ACCOUNT OF ONE
OFFICE MANAGER'S EXPERIENCES WHEN
SHE FOUND HERSELF INVOLVED IN THE
BIZARRE WORLD OF A DYSFUNCTIONAL
HUSBAND AND WIFE DENTAL TEAM

PROLOGUE

I t seemed perfectly fine at first. I was unfamiliar with the dental world from the front desk perspective. The psychiatrist I worked for had recently retired, and this seemed like a good enough replacement. The dentist hired me five minutes after the interview started, and when I reported to work the following day, his first instruction was to cancel all his other interviews. He said he had found Ms. Right for the front desk. From my point of view, I thought this new job could be interesting. There were lots of details to learn because I was unfamiliar with the dental procedures and codes needed for insurance purposes. He took me to lunch that first day and said he was happy he hired me. The next two days were normal enough. I learned the differences between a PPO and a HMO dental plan, how to file the insurance claims, and I became familiar with dental terminology. He didn't have a computer system, and I was just as happy, since I always considered myself not to be very computer savvy.

By the second week, things got a little strange. This nice doctor turned into a foul-mouthed bigot. He termed the HMO patients "vermin" and told me to make them wait at least two weeks for an appointment. He only "watched" cavities instead of filling them. If he waited long enough, the patient would need a crown, and HMOs did not pay participating dentists for cavities—only for crowns.

The PPO patients didn't get treated much better. The dentist made racial slurs all day long, and his language was extremely offensive. He ordered the hygienist to make the cleanings no longer than twenty minutes. This guy was bonkers! I started looking for another job after three months.

My friend Marcie told me she read somewhere that dentists have a very high rate of suicide. She had known some dentists on a personal level and insisted they were all psychological wrecks. I had no firsthand knowledge of this, but I did think this guy was crazy enough to do anything. I found a few other jobs listed for front-desk managers at dental offices. I now felt confident in my understanding of dental procedures and insurance matters, so I thought I would give it another try. Marcie warned me not to apply to another dental office. She encouraged me to seek administrative work elsewhere. I didn't listen, and so began my adventures with *GOING DENTAL in New Jersey.*

THE BEGINNING

Chapter I

Not knowing what I was getting into, I was willing to give working in a dental office another try. I just assumed that the last situation was a fluke, and no other dentist could be as bizarre as the last one. I told myself that Marcie's warnings were unnecessary.

This new ad in the local West Orange New Jersey publication was appealing. It said, "Dental Receptionist needed for small, friendly office." The address was in a house near the corner of Mt. Pleasant Avenue and Crestmont Road. It was about three quarters of a mile from where I lived. I parked in front and thought for a moment about the events that had brought me here. I had moved to the area with my daughter Kimmie after my husband died suddenly of a brain aneurism when Kimmie was just eight years old. He had been a successful insurance broker who never did get around to buying adequate life insurance.

Subsequently, I found myself re-entering the workforce and moving to a more affordable house at a time when Kimmie and I were trying to deal with our grief. Those were trying times, but they were in the past. Working for the psychiatrist had been a rewarding experience. However, that last job at the dental office had been a total disaster. I was ready for a fresh start.

Kimmie was sixteen now, and sometimes, it was not clear which of us had the upper hand. She was very protective of me. It had been just the two of us, until I remarried two years ago, at the age of forty-five. Kimmie liked her stepfather, Bill, just fine. This was Bill's first marriage, and he was more than happy to move into the house that Kimmie and I shared. We gave some thought about moving to a bigger house, but after much discussion, we all decided we liked where we were. Kimmie loved her school and wanted to stay. She was tall and Lanky, just as her father had been. She was pretty, with long dark hair. When Kimmie was younger, she felt awkward about being the tallest girl in her class, and that awkwardness made her quite shy. But now she was happy in her school, and had become more and more outgoing. She was confident enough to play girls' softball and she made a lot of friends on the team. Bill and I did not want to do anything that could trigger her old shyness. I felt very lucky the two of them got along so well. However, Kimmie was still clinging to this little club of her and me. She was used to giving me her opinion about everything.

It was my daughter who encouraged me to answer this new ad for the dental receptionist position. She said I shouldn't be afraid to work in a dental office, just because the last one I worked at was such a disaster. Also, this office was so close to home that I just couldn't pass it up.

I had called and spoken to Dr. Babette Tulip. She told me she and her husband, Dr. Robert Z. Jacobs, were dental partners, and they wanted to meet me as soon as possible.

When I got to the house, I went to the lower level, where there was a separate entrance to the dental office. I walked down a short flight of leaf-covered stairs. In New Jersey, as in all of the Mid-Atlantic States, the holiday season often looks like a picture postcard. The trees outside were nearly stripped of their foliage. The fallen red, brown, and orange leaves covered all of the lawns. There was a definite chill in the air. A Thanksgiving flag waved over the entrance to the office, and inside, there were cute, but tacky, Thanksgiving decorations everywhere.

Dr. Robert Z (for Zachary) Jacobs answered the door to the office. It was after hours, so he wasn't wearing a white coat or dental scrubs. He was a very tall man—I guessed about six feet, four inches. He was average looking, a little out of shape, and probably somewhere in his early thirties. "I'm Lily. I spoke with Dr. Tulip on the phone."

"Yes," he answered. "Dr. Tulip will be right down." He didn't offer me a seat in the waiting room, but instead took a seat behind the front desk, as I remained standing. We spoke for a few minutes about what my duties would be. He didn't seem to mind when I told him I came from an office where there had been no computer.

"We use a software program called Easy Practice," he said. "I'm sure you can learn it. We're a small office. We offer more personal service than some other dental offices. We submit insurance forms for patients, but we don't participate with the insurance companies, and," he continued, "we don't reduce our fees. This allows us to give patients the time they deserve."

Just at that moment, I heard very loud footsteps coming down the stairs to the office from inside the house. A red-haired woman in sweats and high-heeled stilettos appeared. She was small in stature—maybe five feet. She was quite slender and looked as though she worked out often. She wore heavy makeup, and I could tell that her long red hair was a hairpiece attached to medium length hair. It definitely was not the professional hair extensions that many women today wear. I guessed she was somewhere in her early to mid-forties. I thought she could be really attractive, if only she didn't look so false. She was somewhat like the office—cute, but tacky. She came towards me. "You must be Lily. It's so nice to meet you. I'm Dr. Tulip." We exchanged pleasantries. She asked me if I had trouble finding the house.

"No," I answered. "It only took me about five minutes to get here."

As Dr. Tulip and I were talking, I could tell that she was looking me over. I had often been told I looked younger than my years. I had always taken good care of myself, and I had a fairly good figure, even though I was always struggling with five extra pounds. Bill often told me I stood out in a crowd. He said it was the combination of my dark shoulder length hair and green eyes that first caught his attention. But as I was talking to this woman, I got the distinct impression that she didn't like what she was seeing. "Are you married?" Her question surprised me. It didn't seem appropriate for her to ask me such a question less than one minute into the interview. I told her I had been widowed, had a sixteen year old daughter, and had remarried two years ago. With that she said, "Okay," and turned and walked to the back of the office and up the stairs to the main part of the house.

Dr. Jacobs took charge of the interview from there. He did most of the talking and didn't ask many questions. My immediate impression was he liked to hear himself talk. He reiterated many times how he and his wife gave the patients personal service. "We block at least an hour for every patient," he said. "We make appointments on the hour, not on the half-hour. A crown is booked for two hours." He then began to show me the computer program. That was when I heard the soon-to-be familiar footsteps of Dr. Tulip. This time, two darling little boys accompanied her. "These are our boys," she said. "Justin is four and Teddy is two."

"Hi," I said.

"Hi," the older boy responded quietly. His little brother said nothing. With that, Dr. Tulip took each boy by the hand and headed back upstairs.

Dr. Jacobs resumed talking about the computer system for a few more minutes and then started to explain office policy. He told me I did not need to wear scrubs or a lab coat. I was glad to hear that. I liked wearing my own clothes.

We hadn't been talking very long, when Dr. Jacobs stood up. "Okay, I have more interviews to do, I'll call you." I was a little surprised. I was more than qualified for the job. I liked the location, and I was ready to accept the job offer. I didn't realize then that Dr. Jacobs made no decisions without his wife's permission.

During the drive home, I was excited to see my family and tell them about the interview. I was thankful to have Bill in my life. When I was a widow, I missed having a spouse with whom I could share all of the small stuff. Bill was a terrific listener. He was tall, with a great head of dark hair sprinkled with grey. He had an infectious smile and he won my heart soon after we met. One of the things I loved most about Bill was the way he was always interested in the smallest details of both Kimmie's and my life.

When I returned home, I told Bill and Kimmie about the interview. "I think it would be a good office for me to work in," I said. "Dr. Jacobs would be patient with me in learning the computer system. Also, they are a small practice and I could get to really know the patients. The best part is I can wear my own clothes. Dr. Jacobs said he would rather have his front-desk person just dress professionally, not wear a uniform."

Of course, Kimmie picked up on that one. "That's awesome, Mom! I don't picture you in scrubs anyway." Even though in my previous jobs, I had never been asked to wear scrubs, I dreaded finding a job that would require them. I loved clothes, and I loved fashion. I enjoyed picking out an outfit each morning before work. My favorite store was Chico's, and I owned a closet full of their clothes.

I told Bill and Kimmie I was disappointed when Dr. Jacobs didn't hire me immediately. "Don't worry," Kimmie said. "He will."

I got the call the next night. "Can you start on Monday?" I agreed, and the adventure was about to begin.

Chapter 2

I reported to work Monday morning at seven forty-five as planned. The office hours were eight to five, and I was very glad my commute was a short one. The door to the office was left unlocked for me, and I let myself in, hung up my coat, and took my seat behind the front desk. I surveyed my surroundings. The house was at least forty years old. It had always been a dental house. That meant that, from the beginning, there had been a dental office in the basement, with the dentist living upstairs. I believe there is a law that prohibits a medical or dental office to be located in a part of a house, unless the practitioner actually lives in the house. The office was designed by mid-twentieth-century standards. My desk area was actually a square, which reminded me of a little cage. When it was designed, personal computers had not yet been invented, so there was no planned space for one. Of course, I did have a computer at my desk, as well as a fax machine and a credit-card machine. All of this made my area quite crowded. My desk had high counters all around it, so when a patient came in, they could see me only from my shoulders up.

I looked at the appointment book and saw the first patient was not due until nine o'clock. I didn't quite know what to do with myself. No one had come downstairs from the house, so I continued to look around while I waited. There was Thanksgiving stuff all over! The office was overflowing with paper turkeys, pilgrims, and little Thanksgiving bowls with sugarless candy. There were more Thanksgiving decorations than dental posters and pictures. Most dental offices have before and after pictures of teeth. Usually, the walls are decorated with photographs of beautiful people with gorgeous smiles. There was some of that, but not nearly as much as the holiday bric-a-brac.

Dr. Jacobs appeared. This time, he was wearing his lab coat that said, "Dr. Robert Z. Jacobs," above the pocket. "Good morning, Lily." He pulled up a small stool next to my chair at the front desk. He was ready to teach me everything about the office. I must say he was a fairly good teacher. While I knew a lot of the clinical material, codes for procedures, what the different procedures entailed, and how to file insurance claims, I had never used his computer program before. I hadn't grown up with computers. I know that's no excuse. Many people learned how to use them as adults, but it was one of my irrational fears. Computers scared me. I was always afraid I would do something wrong. I knew I needed to get over that, and I was prepared to try. Dr. Jacobs explained things very well. I actually began to feel that the program he used, Easy Practice, was not that complicated.

I noticed he liked to ramble about topics unrelated to dentistry. He talked a lot about football and cars. It didn't matter that I was really lacking in knowledge about those two subjects, as well as being totally uninterested. He continued talking anyway. There were large blocks of time when he just rambled. I simply stared at him and nodded, until he was ready to get back to the dental stuff. I found myself thinking, *Yak, yak, yak,* but he must have thought I was actually listening to the cars and football talk, because it was constant, the entire day, between the office instructions. I wasn't the only one who had to listen to all the football and car talk. Patients got the same treatment. He didn't even ask them if they were interested in the subject. He just started talking about it—mostly about his favorite team—The Washington Redskins. They were his favorite team even though he was originally from Connecticut and now lived in New Jersey. He even followed one patient out the door, because he wasn't finished talking. I thought it was extremely funny. I made a mental note to tell Bill and Kimmie when I got home.

He sat with me between patient appointments that day. He was very thorough in his instructions. I actually felt I was not only understanding the computer program, but also thinking it was easy. The office had a laid-back atmosphere. I liked that. We were closed every day for an hour lunch break. I loved the idea of being able to go home for lunch. It would give me a chance to check on my yellow lab, Beanie, and to watch the first half of my favorite soap, *The Young and the Restless*. I told myself I was lucky to work so close to home. By the end of the first day, I was certain I had landed a great job and would love working there.

Talking to Kimmie and Bill at dinner that night, I tried to explain my day. Kimmie wanted details. I told her I liked Dr. Jacobs but thought he was, in a nice way, a little bit controlling. "He was insistent that all of the pencils and pens on my desk face the same direction in their container, and he didn't want any papers or clutter lying around. I noticed he emptied my recycle bin and wastebasket at least three times that day." I told Bill and Kimmie how Dr. Tulip only saw two patients all day. I went into great detail with my husband and daughter, as I explained. "Dr. Tulip would quickly go upstairs as soon as she was done with a patient. However, she did come downstairs to check on us several times during the day."

Bill was a little less than excited about my new job. "Are you sure you want this?" he asked.

"Why are you asking me this?" I replied.

"Well, they seem a little strange to me, but if you like it there, it's your call."

Back at the office, I soon learned a multiple of facts about my new surroundings. Dr. Jacobs did all of the restorative work—fillings, crowns, bridges, and dentures. Dr. Tulip did all of the recalls—or cleanings. He told me she had been a dental hygienist for several years before she went to dental school, and she still liked to do all of the cleanings. I later learned that they met in dental school and she was several years older than him. Dr. Jacobs also told me his wife had been divorced twice before he met her. At first, I felt somewhat shocked when he told me so much personal information, but I dismissed it as being just his blabbermouth personality.

It soon became apparent that Dr. Tulip did not like to do any of the real dental work. When she was cleaning a patient's teeth and found an area of decay, she would instruct me. "Make an appointment and put them on Dr. Jacobs' side." She did so little of the actual dentistry, I wondered why she had even bothered to become a dentist. She spent most of her day upstairs. She only came downstairs when I called to announce her recall (cleaning and exam) patient had arrived. She always appeared wearing full makeup and high heels. She wore a lab coat over her clothes, but when she was finished with her patient and took the lab coat off, she was usually wearing clothes that teenagers today would describe as "hot." I often thought she was an attractive woman, but with no sense of style. I believed she could look really good, if she would only tone things down a bit and dress appropriately.

Dr. Tulip, in my opinion, was "phony baloney" all the way. She always greeted her patients by saying, "Hiii, I gotta tell you, you look terrific." She was a great schmoozer. She could make a patient believe she empathized with whatever they were going through at the moment. If a patient had a child about to graduate, whether it was from high school or college, she could go on and on about it, treating it like it was the most important event in the world. She did her cleanings very fast, talking all the while. She seemed a little sugary sweet to me, but she had quite a few patients who really loved her and felt she understood them. She really did have a certain way about her. She schmoozed in a much different manner than did Dr. Jacobs. She was always sure to talk about something that interested the patient. She could make them feel like she was a perfect listener. I could always tell it was an act and just part of her persona. I didn't think she really cared about the details of her patients' lives.

She didn't say much to me, other than the usual pleasantries, such as "Good morning, how was your weekend?" She was always in a hurry to get back upstairs. Justin was in pre-school and Teddy was too young for school. Maria, the full time housekeeper, was there every day from six o'clock in the morning until seven o'clock at night. Yet Dr. Tulip seemed to prefer being upstairs rather than downstairs practicing dentistry.

Dr. Jacobs was a different story. He ran every aspect of the office. He was at my desk between patients and sometimes during patients. While doing his restorations, he would often say to the patient, "I will be right back." He required constant breaks. Several times during the day, he would check the front desk to make sure everything was in order. He wanted to know the purpose of every stray paper and what every phone call was about. He was forever arranging my pencils. He seemed to talk just to hear the sound of his own voice. Several times during the day, I would stop whatever I was doing and just stare at him, while he talked about anything and everything. He didn't seem tuned into whether or not I was truly listening. This man could really yak. One of his habits was quite annoying. Sometimes, while he was yakking away, he would squeeze and pop zits on his arm or face. I could hardly believe my eyes the first time he did that in front of me. I was repulsed but couldn't stop myself from looking. Yes, Dr. Jacobs certainly was unusual, but somehow I trusted him. He seemed lost and truly in need of someone to listen to him. Something about him made me believe he was honest.

There were actually a lot of positives in that office. As the days wore on, I got to really know and like the patients. I dealt with many nice families. The patients appreciated never being rushed, and there was always time for emergencies. The days were rarely booked completely. If someone broke a tooth or woke up with an infection, I could always fit him or her in. Also, if we had a cancellation, or if we were finished early, I could go home. I loved that. I felt the job had a lot of flexibility and that suited me just fine. They were the friendly neighborhood dentists. But one never really fully knows what goes on in one's own neighborhood.

Chapter 3

I became quite an expert on dental matters. I thought of myself as a "virtual dentist." I knew what every procedure was about. When a patient called, I would always forward their questions to Dr. Jacobs, but I began to notice that I usually knew what the answer would be. I learned in detail all aspects of dental insurance. I did the accounts receivable and payable. I still had some trouble with the computer, when it didn't do exactly what I wanted it to do. Dr. Jacobs was extremely helpful at those times. He was always available to answer all of my questions. I was grateful for that.

I enjoyed my job. However, it soon became apparent to me that both Dr. Jacobs and Dr. Tulip were extremely neurotic, and at times, they were rather hostile to each other. He was compulsive beyond compare. At least three times a day, he would go behind my desk and empty my recycle bin, looking at every paper I threw away. If I made a mistake with something, I didn't want him looking through the trash and finding it. More than once, I actually stuffed some trash into my purse. I would plan to throw it away later when I got home. I really felt uncomfortable that

Dr. Jacobs would see my mistakes and question me about them. I couldn't believe I was actually stuffing trash into my purse, but I really felt it was my only alternative.

The constant chatter continued all day long. It wasn't just to me. As soon as a patient got in his chair, he would start. It was never just, "How are you, Mrs. Jones, let's get right to your filling." It was always about cars, sports, or him. He didn't care whether the patient was interested or not. I often wondered why patients didn't set him straight. It was physically a very small office, and I had a clear view of his operatory. Sometimes, Dr. Jacobs would actually put down his instruments, stand up, and yak for ten minutes or so. More than once, when a patient would pay at the front desk, they would mention they were late getting back to work. They usually announced this while rolling their eyes.

Dr. Tulip was entirely different. I thought she was rather hyper. When she was downstairs, she would go from room to room, always looking for stuff, always asking Dr. Jacobs where some instrument or other piece of equipment could be found. She was totally clueless as to what went on at the front desk. She wanted patients to like her. It probably would be more accurate to say she wanted patients to worship her. She complimented them beyond reason. She also gave gifts to her favorite patients. She would frequently present them with a scarf, a purse, whatever she felt like giving away. She usually said someone had given the item to her and she either already had one or just couldn't use it.

There was a group of women patients who really loved this. The things that Dr. Tulip gave away were nice—some of it designer. She sometimes told patients not to worry about paying for some of the services she performed.

Occasionally, when she was cleaning someone's teeth, she did a little extra bonding, or whitening, or whatever she felt like doing that day. She would then tell me not to charge them. This royal treatment was only for a select few. It drove Dr. Jacobs crazy. He complained to me how she was giving services away—even for patients who had dental insurance. Some of the procedures she performed would have been paid for by insurance, so it didn't make sense not to charge the patients. I started to suspect Dr. Tulip of trying to mask her poor dentistry. Patients were so busy thinking she was their true buddy, they overlooked some of her inadequate work. She was great at cleaning teeth, but every time she consented to do a filling or any other real dentistry, it would take her an extra-long time, and she constantly asked for help from her husband. Perhaps, I concluded, she hoped that her patients would love her so much that they wouldn't notice she was not even completing their work by herself.

Dr. Tulip wanted to be a best friend to all of her patients. I sometimes felt like cringing when she crossed the line. I remember the day the Amy Mavery situation came up. Amy was a difficult patient. She was very demanding and often rescheduled her appointments at the last minute. Dr. Tulip was very selective as to whom she liked and didn't like. For reasons only known to Dr. Tulip, she liked Amy Mavery. When Dr. Tulip liked a patient, she lost any professionalism she might have had and gave them special treatment. She told Amy she could have a thirty-percent discount on her two crowns. Dr. Jacobs was going to do the crowns, so he was furious when Dr. Tulip had promised this to Amy. Anyway, since Dr. Tulip had promised this, I had to honor it, and Amy got her discount. Dr. Jacobs and Dr. Tulip argued about it for the rest of the day. They tossed each other dirty looks at every opportunity, and he was at my desk every chance he got, complaining about his wife. "What is she thinking? You can't just arbitrarily give discounts to patients." And so it went, on and on the rest of the day. As usual, I stayed out of it. However, I really thought it was bad for the practice to give discounts at random. This wasn't a case of need. It was just Dr. Tulip trying to buy the patient's love.

Three days later, a letter came. It was from Amy Mavery's husband. It went something like this: "Thank you for giving my wife the thirty-percent discount. It's really appreciated. However, I had two crowns done eighteen months ago, and you did not offer me a discount. Below, find an itemized bill requesting that you refund thirty percent of the fee that was charged me."

Needless to say, the two docs had another huge argument that day. "Babette, what in the world were you thinking? I'll be damned if I'll give that jerk any money! Why in the world did you offer her that discount?" Dr. Tulip could not be reprimanded for any reason. Challenging her was like waving red in front of a bull. And so it escalated. They continued screaming at each other between patients. In the end, I was called upon to write a letter to Amy's husband, telling him he was not entitled to a discount. We lost both of them as patients. I told Dr. Jacobs later, "You can make your friends patients, but it was unprofessional to make your patients your friends." I couldn't help but think how Dr. Tulip must be very needy to resort to bribery to make her patients like her. Giving unreasonable discounts for no reason, showering lavish gifts on patients, I felt, was all very inappropriate.

Dr. Jacobs also did things I found questionable. Thomas Caper was one of my favorite patients. He was an exceedingly pleasant man and always seemed to take any recommended suggestions Dr. Jacobs made. Thomas had some old silver fillings on his molars. Dr. Jacobs told him he should replace these old "amalgams" with composite (or white) fillings. This is a common practice in many dental offices—to replace silver fillings with white ones for cosmetic reasons. Of course, many offices don't tell the patient that, if the fillings are deep, there is always a chance of damaging the nerve, and then a root canal and crown would be necessary. For this reason, just as many offices will wait until the fillings are chipped or leaking before replacing them.

Thomas was a nice-looking man, and I'm sure he felt such a move would enhance his smile. Anyway, Thomas agreed, and Dr. Jacobs, during a lengthy visit, replaced the old silver fillings with new white ones. The next day, Thomas called. He was in excruciating pain. I found room in the schedule for him that afternoon. Dr. Jacobs said the x-rays looked fine, and the pain was probably temporary. He told Thomas to wait a few days and then report back. In a few days, Thomas had a major infection. Dr. Jacobs put him on antibiotics. The pain continued. Thomas reported it was agonizing. So Dr. Jacobs then referred him to Dr. Steiner, the endodontist. Dr. Steiner did two root canals on Thomas and then referred him back to our office for crowns. Whenever there is a root canal, a crown must be placed to protect the tooth.

Poor Thomas! The whole affair took weeks. It was a week to let the root canals heal, then the teeth had to be prepped for crowns and the temporary crowns placed.

It was another two weeks before the permanent crowns came back from the lab. Also, Thomas had suffered with the pain and infection at least two weeks prior to the root canals. Scenarios like this happen in dental offices all the time. However, Thomas had been talked into having the silver fillings replaced. The old fillings may have needed to be replaced in the future, but to do it now was strictly cosmetic. That is a viable choice for some patients, but Thomas did not really come in looking for that. Technically, Dr. Jacobs had done nothing wrong. But I couldn't help but feel he had pushed this cosmetic procedure when Thomas was not really very interested, and the risks had not been fully explained to the patient.

Anyway, the bill was extensive. I told Dr. Jacobs he needed to reduce the bill substantially. Dr. Jacobs did not agree with me and told me to bill Thomas Caper the full amount. He insisted his time was valuable, and replacing the fillings was a reasonable thing to do. I kept thinking how Dr. Jacobs was just terrible at reading people. I knew he would lose Thomas as a patient if he did not adjust the bill. Thomas had already paid for the fillings and half of the crowns. I did as I was told and billed him for the remainder. Weeks passed and we received no payment. Dr. Jacobs told me to call him and ask what the problem was. I *knew* what the problem was. I followed orders and called Thomas. He sent the check in, but we never saw him and his family again. Dr. Jacobs was so stubborn that he lost the whole family as patients. He could be extremely unreasonable at times. Furthermore, he kept insisting to me how replacing the crowns was really his wife's idea. I got the impression that behind the scenes, Dr. Tulip was always telling Dr. Jacobs to schedule more and more procedures.

Of course, it didn't excuse Dr. Jacobs from following his wife's urging, even when he knew in his heart that some of these procedures could certainly wait.

Every time a patient left the practice, it was a big deal. The two docs would blame each other. It was a small practice, and we couldn't afford to have patients leave. Of course, patients leave for many reasons, and it is normal to lose a percentage of patients every year. However, most practices acquire new patients every month to offset any patient vacancies. We did get some new patients, but not nearly enough. The patient base kept decreasing. I didn't know for sure whether it was Dr. Jacobs' constant yakking or the dirty looks between the two dentists, but it seemed to me we were starting to lose an unusual amount of patients.

One morning, both docs were standing near me when a patient called to have her records forwarded to another dentist. That was the first time I witnessed a serious argument between Dr. Jacobs and Dr. Tulip.

"It's your fault!" she screamed at him.

"What do you mean *my* fault?" he screamed back at her.

"I told you before, and I guess I have to tell you again, you didn't handle that last crown right."

He was getting red in the face. "Babette, as usual you don't know what you're talking about."

"SHUT UP!" she screamed at him really loudly, then she turned and went upstairs. He mumbled under his breath, "Fuck you," as he ran after her. I could then hear arguing going on upstairs, but I couldn't make out the words.

It was a good thing there were no patients for that hour slot. He came down about twenty minutes later and announced to me that his wife was an idiot. "She knows nothing about dentistry, let alone about running a practice." I was really uncomfortable with all of this. I now knew the tension I had been sensing between the two of them was not only real but far worse than I thought.

That night at dinner, I told Bill and Kimmie what had happened. They both thought I was working in a rather bizarre atmosphere. "Look Lily, enough is enough." Bill was adamant. "You can find a job that's not as stressful as this one. Those two dentists sound like nut jobs."

"But I'm not ready to give up," I protested. "I know it sounds strange, but it's interesting there. I like the patients and, while I sometimes feel uncomfortable when they fight, it's rather exciting to see what will happen next."

"Bill is right." Kimmie agreed with her stepfather. "That is one weird environment."

None of us knew how right they would turn out to be.

* * *

Chapter 4

Robert and Babette were upstairs in the family room, watching television with the kids. The day's events had been exasperating for Robert. He had seen many patients that day, and he had worked exceedingly hard. He was feeling rather depressed. Two patients had asked to have their records transferred. "You know, Babette. I think I did my best, but patients don't really appreciate that. We lost another two, today."

Babette looked at him with disdain. "Of course they left. It's you!"

He could feel his face getting flushed. He attempted to answer her charges. "What do you mean, it's me? I really try downstairs. You, on the other hand, won't even attempt to do the hard cases. I do everything."

"You do not do everything." She didn't miss a beat. "I work hard upstairs and downstairs. I take care of the kids. I take care of the house. If patients are leaving, it's because you give them lousy care. You know what, Robert? Your work is lousy!"

He was not to be outdone. His temper was quickly rising. "What do you mean, *you* do everything? Last time I looked, we had a housekeeper."

She gave him one more dirty look and then practically dragged Justin and Teddy upstairs and put them to bed. He changed the channel to a sports event and tried to relax. About twenty minutes later, she came downstairs and turned off the TV, just as an exciting play was about to happen. "What the hell are you doing?" he screamed at her.

"You don't deserve to watch TV!" she said. She was vicious in her attack. "You don't deserve to have a wonderful wife like me! You're a total loser!"

"Don't you call me a loser, you bitch!" he quickly retorted. "You spend every cent I make!"

The argument was escalating to a fevered pitch. Something told her she'd better stop. She went into the kitchen and took out a bottle of liquor. She took it upstairs with her. When he later came up to the room, she was passed out on top of the covers. He got in the bed and went to sleep. In the middle of the night, she woke up and started to grope him. "You really are a bitch you know," he said, and then they enjoyed the best sex they'd had in weeks.

＊ ＊ ＊

Chapter 5

I was starting to question the type of work that was coming out of the practice. I was beginning to feel that some of the patients were not getting the best of care.

Michael Lister was a nice man. He worked as an assistant manager of a bank, and he was always friendly when I saw him. He came in for a cleaning. At the end of it, Dr. Tulip called Dr. Jacobs to come into the operatory. "I just told Michael his four front teeth are severely damaged. He grinds his teeth, and they are very badly worn down. It is affecting his bite. He needs to have ten veneers. What do you think?" Dr. Jacobs was a little surprised. He examined Michael's teeth. The front four anterior teeth really could benefit from veneers. Certainly, they would improve Michael's appearance. He motioned to his wife to join him in the back room. "Michael, we will be right back."

"Babette, what exactly are you talking about? I could see four veneers as probable, but ten?"

"Don't be stupid, Robert," she countered. "He has a very wide smile. When he grins, you can see all ten. If you want them to match, he needs ten veneers." Dr. Jacobs knew that ten veneers were totally unnecessary. The standard procedure would have been to place six veneers at the most. However, Babette Tulip had that look in her eye. He knew not to cross her. Against all of his instincts and professional training, he followed her back into the operatory where Michael Lister was waiting.

"Well, Michael, Dr. Tulip is right. You really do need ten veneers. Anything less would be insufficient. Your smile would not look right." He looked over at his wife, who had a very knowing, smug look on her face.

Michael Lister was a man who believed everything his doctors told him. He easily believed what the two dentists were telling him. It sounded logical, and he cared about his appearance. He was quite surprised when he learned the fee for veneers was one thousand dollars per tooth. However, he really did care about his teeth. He had connections at the bank where he worked, and he was confident he could secure a low interest loan. He made an appointment to have the work done.

* * *

That night, upstairs in their bedroom, Robert brought the subject up. "Babette, I'm really not totally comfortable with the Lister case."

"Why not?" She snapped back.

"He doesn't need ten veneers. He only needs four. Also, I assume you want me to do the work. I don't want to do ten."

"You are such a wimp!" she screamed. "What is wrong with you? It's ten thousand dollars, Robert, ten thousand dollars!" She screamed this at him while she dropped her robe. She was naked underneath. He threw her down on the bed. "Ten veneers," he whispered.

* * *

At Michael Lister's next appointment, Dr. Jacobs did all the work, with Dr. Tulip in the room the whole time, trying to tell him what to do. It was always amazing to me that Dr. Tulip, who actually didn't do any real dentistry, always thought she knew better than Dr. Jacobs how to do every procedure. It was a two-hour appointment. Michael Lister came out to the front desk to pay. I didn't think his temporary veneers looked good at all, but he was to come back in two weeks to have the permanent ones put on. He would just have to wear the temporary ones, while the lab was making the permanent ones from the impressions Dr. Jacobs had just taken. Michael seemed somewhat satisfied. He told me he was hopeful the permanent veneers would look great. He paid his bill and left.

I didn't feel good about the Lister case. I had an uneasy feeling. Michael came back in two weeks at the appointed time to have the permanent veneers put on. The final result looked better than the temporaries, but I actually thought his teeth now resembled big "Chiclets." Dr. Tulip went on and on about how wonderful they looked. Dr. Jacobs told Michael he now had a great smile. Michael seemed to like them well enough. However, the complications were about to begin.

Within two days, the veneers started to fall off. Mostly it was on the sides. It was on the teeth that Dr. Jacobs had doubts about doing. Michael needed to come in at least six times in the next two weeks to have the veneers cemented back on. "Why are these veneers constantly falling off?" He asked Dr. Jacobs. Dr. Jacobs had all kinds of excuses, but I could tell that Michael Lister was becoming really aggravated. Michael was having so much trouble with these veneers that Dr. Jacobs told him the only way to correct the ones that were falling off was to make crowns on those teeth. Crowns would offer full coverage and protection. They would be like little gloves that fit over each tooth. Veneers were just protection on the front of the teeth. Crowns were the way to go.

Surprisingly, Michael listened, and so began a grueling process of Michael having Dr. Jacobs replace the troubling veneers with crowns. Dr. Jacobs did not offer to do the crowns for free. He just subtracted the cost of the veneers from the crowns. The difference was about three hundred dollars per tooth, so Michael still owed several hundred dollars, in addition to the money he had already paid for the veneers. Surprisingly, Michael agreed, and then the situation went from bad to worse. The crowns, once placed, didn't feel right. Michael wanted his money back, so he could go to another dentist and "have these teeth fixed right," he said.

The two docs argued. "You are not giving him one dollar back." Dr. Tulip was irate. "Let him go someplace else. Who cares? You did what was necessary. If he's not happy, it's his problem."

Dr. Jacobs really did feel bad. He felt guilty because he had listened, against his better judgment, to his wife. He had tried his best. He knew those side teeth would not hold veneers, but he'd done the work anyway. He couldn't stand it when Babette badgered him. He had given in. He only hoped that, somehow, it would all work out.

Of course, I had to listen to Dr. Jacobs' constant complaining about the situation. "I shouldn't have listened to her, Lily. I knew it was a mistake from the very beginning. Veneers should never have been placed on those side teeth."

"So why did you do it?" I asked. Dr. Jacobs gave me one of his "looks." I had grown to know that look. It meant— "What choice did I really have. She insisted that I do it." I never could figure that one out completely—why he was so afraid to cross his wife.

* * *

Michael Lister had reached the end of his patience. He had trusted Dr. Jacobs and Dr. Tulip when they told him he needed ten veneers. He was now in the waiting room of a well-known malpractice attorney. He wanted to sue for enough money to repair the damage they had done to his teeth.

"What do you think? Do I have a case against those two? I've spent over ten thousand dollars on these damn veneers, not to mention the additional money I had to shell out for the lousy crowns, and all I have is trouble and pain? I spoke with Dr. Barry Rosenstein. This time I checked. This guy is highly rated. I should have checked better before I went to those other quacks. He can re-do my teeth. Trouble is, though, it's going to cost me—somewhere around twenty grand. Do I have a case or not?"

The lawyer listened to Michael very carefully. He spoke with him for nearly an hour. At the end of the consultation, what the lawyer had to say was not what Michael wanted to hear. "Mr. Lister, it does seem as though you were treated very poorly, but I have to advise you that this case will be very hard to prove. It is extremely difficult to get a malpractice judgment under these circumstances, especially when the dentist who did the work is offering to keep repairing it. We can proceed with the suit, but you probably will not win, and you will still have legal fees to contend with."

Michael was distraught. Somehow he would get the money to let Dr. Rosenstein repair his teeth. He would contact that awful office of Jacobs and Tulip and have his records sent to Dr. Rosenstein's office.

* * *

It was about six months later, when I read in the newspaper that Michael Lister had been arrested for embezzling twenty thousand dollars from the bank where he worked.

I showed the article to Dr. Jacobs and Dr. Tulip. They were shocked, but they didn't show any compassion. I wondered out loud whether Michael had stolen the money because of his teeth. I suspected that was the case. They both pretended not to see any connection at all. These people were always so caught up in the trivia of their own lives that there was never any room for concern for others.

Bill and Kimmie were amazed. "Do you think he stole the money because of his dental work?" Kimmie was really into this.

"That would be my guess," I answered. "Michael Lister was such a nice guy. The whole thing is really upsetting."

"Sure can't say you work in a dull place," was Bill's only response.

However, later that evening, when Bill and I were upstairs in our room, Bill wanted to revisit the entire issue. "Face it, Lily, you work for a quack. You need to quit, and quit now!"

"No I don't," I quickly responded. "I know it's a little strange over there, but I like the patients, and Dr. Jacobs and I get along just fine. It's him and his crazy wife who don't get along."

"That's my point, exactly," Bill persisted. "Look at the facts, Lily. This guy is supposed to be a professional, yet he does whatever his incompetent wife tells him to do. He messed up Michael Lister's teeth and didn't take any responsibility for it. I can't figure out why you can't see what's right before your eyes."

I was getting really fired up by that time. "What's right before my eyes," I shot back, "is you telling me what to do and I don't like it one bit!"

Later that night, I lay awake and thought about everything. I had been very angry with Bill for practically ordering me to quit. I asked myself whether I was really angry at Bill or if I was just angry at myself for staying at that job, when I knew he was right and was only looking out for me. Also, I had been a completely independent woman before Bill came into my life. It was unacceptable to me that he thought he could tell me what I should do about my job. Then again, I knew he loved me and was concerned. Bill was ordinarily not bossy. I knew this. If I could be totally honest with myself, I would have to admit that I, too, had some of the same concerns.

Chapter 6

Dr. Jacobs was now constantly complaining about Dr. Tulip. That really troubled me. These people were married. I didn't want to be in the middle of their problems. However, there was no stopping him. He complained about his wife's refusal to even try to do most restorative work. He hated how she gave services away as well as other gifts. He felt she was undermining the financial well being of the practice. She had no rhyme or reason for the way she randomly gave out discounts. She wanted patients to think she was the most sympathetic person in the world. In reality, she was phony all the way. On the wall behind my desk were their diplomas and certificates. One award was given to Dr. Tulip in dental school for "most friendly." She actually told me she had been upset by that award. "Why?" I asked.

"Because my work was outstanding," she answered. "I don't want an award for being friendly. Who cares? I wanted one for my work." That about summed up Dr. Tulip—fake friendliness and illusions of superiority when it came to her work.

She had the following of a group of women who only wanted her to do their restorative work, and they didn't like it when she told them Dr. Jacobs would do it. For this group of women, she sometimes agreed to do the restorations. Each time I booked one of these appointments, I thought the patient would one day regret his or her decision. Dr. Tulip did not know what she was doing. Invariably, she would call Dr. Jacobs in to help her finish a procedure. She would make up some excuse to the patient, go into Dr. Jacobs' operatory, and tell him he needed to come into her room immediately. He would have to interrupt whatever he was doing and finish her job, or at least make corrections to it. I don't know what her patients were thinking, but she seemed to have them convinced they were getting the very best of care. The real kicker was when Dr. Tulip did have one of these patients, Dr. Jacobs ended up actually doing most of the work. Then, Dr. Tulip would say the rest of the day, "Wow, did you see the crowns on Mrs. Jones? Weren't they terrific? I know I did a really fabulous job on those." Dr. Tulip could certainly sing her own praises.

Always, after one of these episodes, Dr. Jacobs would spend the rest of the day at my desk complaining about his wife. He was angry that she didn't try to master important, essential techniques. He complained she was always in a rush and would make things up as she went along. "She knows the right way to do things," he would complain. "She doesn't follow the necessary steps. In dentistry, there are proven ways to do things. She skips around and thinks she can do whatever she wants." As usual, I would just stare at him and think, *yak, yak, yak. Why don't you take it up with her? What do you want me to do about it?*

Dr. Tulip had her own grievances. She started to open up to me a little more—but never to the extent her husband did. She complained he was controlling, bossy, and hard to live with. This I believed. The man truly was a control freak. I often noticed how frequently they interrupted each other and threw each other dirty looks during the day.

The tension between the two of them became the usual topic at dinner with Bill and Kimmie. My daughter seemed to relish hearing the office gossip. Bill would usually mumble something about my finding another job. I wasn't ready for that. I actually liked my job. I could tolerate the two crazy docs. They were both civil to me, and it was rather interesting in a weird sort of way. I loved my short commute. The pay was decent. Most of all, I had a lot of flexibility. Bill was a CPA. He belonged to a lot of professional organizations, and he attended meetings out of state at least four times a year. I liked to go with him. It was not a problem in my office. Dr. Jacobs had assured me I could do this. I didn't want to go to another situation where taking time off for travel wouldn't be possible. And so it continued—Dr. Jacobs talking all day long about anything that popped into his head, but especially about his wife and her lack of professionalism, and Dr. Tulip— buttering up patients, bribing them with gifts, and giving Dr. Jacobs angry glances at frequent intervals during the day.

I got very used to Dr. Jacobs and his compulsive ways. Even in his weirdness, he was always nice to me. He told me many times he liked having me there. He often said, "Please do not quit on me." I thought that was rather strange, but then again, he probably knew that not many people could tolerate working for a dentist who talked about his personal problems all day.

Dr. Tulip had her moments. She was as changeable as the weather. When she felt like it, she would stop by my desk and be very friendly. Other times, she would be extremely cold—almost like I was one of the fixtures. If there was something she didn't like, she never confronted me but had Dr. Jacobs do it. One day, as I was checking a patient out at the front desk, I said, "Finished already?" I didn't think anything at all about saying that. I was just being friendly to the patient. However, the next morning, I heard from Dr. Jacobs how Dr. Tulip was not pleased with what I had said. I asked him why. He said she complained that it made her sound as though she cleaned the patient's teeth too fast and thus did not do a thorough job. I thought she was being overly picky. I soon learned that Dr. Tulip was always listening and putting her own interpretations on things. I did not trust her. I always had the feeling she tolerated me because she knew Dr. Jacobs liked me, and since he actually ran the office, I was there to stay. She also was extremely moody. One never knew what to expect from her—overly friendly one day, cold the next. Dr. Jacobs seemed to tiptoe around her, but he always seemed as though he was just about at the boiling point. He could tiptoe around her for only so long—and then he would say something sarcastic, and the fighting would follow.

In the beginning, they generally took their fights upstairs. More and more, however, there were times when they both stood in front of my desk and fought. Of course, that was when no patients were there, but it was extremely awkward for me. The arguments were really quite trivial. Perhaps Dr. Jacobs had interrupted Dr. Tulip while she was talking, or worse still, he disagreed with her evaluation of a patient. She really didn't want his opinion, but she would ask him anyway. Then, when he told her what he thought, there would be an explosion.

As controlling as Dr. Jacobs was, I felt comfortable around him. His people skills were not the greatest. If they had been, he would know when to stop yakking. I really liked the way no computer question I asked him was ever too stupid. I didn't mind how he always wanted to know what was going on at the front desk. It was a "checks and balances" system for me, and it actually made me more comfortable in the job.

And so it was—me in that rather strange office, but actually liking my job. As every holiday approached, Dr. Tulip would bring out the flags and decorations. There were Easter bunnies, Halloween goblins, Christmas Santas, and St. Patrick's Day flags. Each holiday was a big deal at the office. Dr. Tulip always spent more energy decorating the office than in fixing people's teeth. When she wasn't decorating the office with endless "do-dads," she was upstairs, either exercising or cooking. Dr. Jacobs was always complaining to me how his wife wasn't putting any effort into the dental practice, and I was always protesting that he should be talking to her and not me about his complaints. She was extremely moody and he was extremely compulsive. Looking back on it now, I didn't realize how severe their problems were.

I really enjoyed the contact I had with the patients. I knew them well and they all knew me. I liked it when they would call and say, "Hi, Lily, I was hoping you could fit me in tomorrow." The general atmosphere was pleasant, unless Dr. Jacobs and Dr. Tulip were next to each other. At those times, I could feel the tension. There were constant dirty looks going on between the two of them. It seemed to me he was always "walking on eggs" when he talked to her. The tone of his voice, or any hint of him telling her what to do would offend her. I always had great stories to tell Bill and Kimmie when I got home. But one Thanksgiving weekend, I had no idea that the strangest story of all was about to unfold.

Chapter 7

It was a Wednesday afternoon, the day before Thanksgiving. I had been working at the office of Jacobs and Tulip, DDS, for two years. It was hard to believe so much time had actually gone by. Kimmie was in college, now, but she was expected home that night for the holiday. Bill would be picking her up from the airport, while I prepared for Thanksgiving dinner.

As usual, the office was overflowing with holiday decorations. There were lots of paper turkeys, pilgrim candy dishes with sugar-free candy, and all kinds of fall leaf decorations. The last two years had seen countless decorations for every single holiday. I had witnessed two years of changeable pilgrims, Santas, and bunnies. I had dealt with hanging mobile hearts swinging near my face in February. Now I was looking at paper pilgrims adorning my desk. I actually thought of them now as tacky, but the holiday decorations continued, as did the tension between the two dentists.

I thought the strain between the two was zapping the office of energy. They seemed to fight about everything. There were many fights about relatives. They seemed to hate each other's families. Dr. Tulip made no secret of her disdain for Dr. Jacobs' mother, who was about to come visit from Connecticut. The two of them were becoming very predictable in their fights. One of them would casually say something that would anger the other. They would start to argue and then say, "Let's take this upstairs." They would go upstairs, and a lot of yelling would start. Sometimes, I could make out what was being said, but not always. Dr. Jacobs' voice was very loud. He would be screaming. Her voice was more muffled. However, I knew whatever was being said up there was not pretty.

I worried about the boys. They were not always in school when these arguments were going on. I didn't think it was right for these children to be exposed to all of that yelling, but I didn't know what exactly I could do about it. Sometimes, they would have one of their fights in the morning and then, after lunch, they would be talking to each other like nothing even happened. It was amazing to me the way they could turn things off and on. This particular week had been bad. They were jumping all over each other for everything. The tension was especially thick all week, but I had no idea just how tense things could actually get.

I went home that Wednesday night looking forward to a nice Thanksgiving, and that's exactly what we had. The weekend was fun and relaxing. I truly enjoyed having Kimmie home, even though I didn't get to spend as much time with her as I would have liked. She wanted to see all of her old high school friends, so she was out and about most of the time.

* * *

Robert's mother was visiting from Connecticut for Thanksgiving weekend. Babette Tulip hated her mother-in-law. The feeling was mutual. Helen Jacobs was proud of her son. He had never disappointed her. Never, that is, until he married that money-hungry, man-eating woman. She wondered many times, *Why did he marry a woman so much older than himself?* It wasn't just the age difference that bothered Helen. It was almost everything about her daughter-in-law. The woman always had to be right. No matter what the issue, Babette's opinion was the only one that mattered. Helen loved her grandchildren. Justin and Teddy gave her great joy. However, Babette controlled everything. There had been times when Helen wasn't even allowed to see her grandchildren, let alone talk to them on the phone. It seemed that Babette blamed Helen for a lot of the marital problems between herself and Robert. She constantly accused Robert of listening to his mother more than to her. Because of that, whenever Babette and Robert had an argument, Babette did her best to make sure the children had no contact with their grandmother.

Thanksgiving Dinner was fairly uneventful. Helen thought Babette had a few too many glasses of wine. She decided not to say anything about it. She was trying, at least on her part, to make this a pleasant weekend. The atmosphere changed later that night when Helen went upstairs and headed toward the guest room. Babette and the children had gone upstairs hours ago. Helen assumed they were asleep. However, when she walked past the master bedroom, she could see past the half-opened door. Babette was asleep on top of the covers. Teddy and Justin were sleeping next to her. Helen pushed the door open and walked up to the bed. She could smell the liquor on

Babette's breath. There was a half empty bottle of scotch on the bedside table. The whole scene infuriated Helen. Her grandchildren were asleep on the bed next to their passed-out, drunken mother.

"Babette, Babette, wake up." Helen shook her daughter-in-law several times. "Get up and put these boys in their own beds. They shouldn't be seeing you like this." Babette was startled awake. "What the hell are you doing? Get the hell out of my bedroom!" With that, she jumped out of the bed and began pushing Helen. "You interfering old woman, how dare you come into my bedroom and tell me what do!"

The boys were shocked awake. It was a terrible scene for them to witness. Babette continued screaming at her mother-in-law, all the while, trying to push her out of the room. Helen fell down, and her daughter-in-law pounced on top of her, grabbed the older woman's shoulders and shook her violently. Robert heard all the screaming and ran upstairs. When he got to the master bedroom, he found his wife on top of his mother. Both women were shouting at each other. The boys were crying and trying to stop the fight. Robert yanked his wife by her ponytail and lifted her off of his mother. Everyone stood there for a moment in shock. Then Babette grabbed her car keys, which were lying on the dresser. Teddy was the closest boy to her. She grabbed him and ran into the garage. Moments later, she took off with Teddy in the car.

She didn't get very far. She was driving erratically and was pulled over. Not only was she drunk, but also she was endangering a child. The police officer called for backup. After Teddy was returned home, Babette Tulip was taken down to the police station and booked. Robert fully intended to let her stay there.

The night, however, was not yet over. After Babette's own mother bailed her out, Babette accused her husband of spousal abuse. A warrant was issued for his arrest. Robert Jacobs was awakened when two policemen came to his house and arrested him in front of his mother and his children.

* * *

I drove to the office on Monday morning, refreshed from my holiday weekend. I could never imagine what was waiting for me inside.

The door was locked. That was quite unusual. One of the doctors usually got up in the morning and opened the office. I possessed an office key, but I had never used it. I often told them I would be glad to open up in the morning—turning on lights and the office music, but for some reason they liked to do those tasks themselves. So, it was really strange when, after the Thanksgiving weekend, the door was locked. I pulled out my office key and let myself in. I had just turned on the lights, when I heard Dr. Jacobs' footsteps on the back stairs. "Lily," he said, "lock the door to the office. We're not open for business today. I need to tell you what happened."

"What! What happened?" I practically screamed. My curiosity was at record levels, and I sensed that something was dreadfully wrong. "Dr. Tulip is gone. She's at her mother's house in Teaneck."

He then proceeded to tell me about the horrific chain of events that followed Thanksgiving dinner. "You know Dr. Tulip is an alcoholic don't you?"

"No," I said. "I know she's moody, but I've never seen her drunk, and you've never said anything about her being an alcoholic."

"Well she is, and she put away quite a few at Thanksgiving dinner and all through the evening." I stood there dumbfounded and listened. I didn't really want to be involved, but I also couldn't help myself from standing there and just hearing it.

While Dr. Jacobs was describing the Thanksgiving disaster, I kept thinking how strange it was that he kept referring to his wife as Dr. Tulip. He was talking about really personal things and he kept calling her "Dr. Tulip," instead of "Babette." In the office they always referred to each other as Dr. Jacobs and Dr. Tulip, and they never asked me to call them by their first names, even when there were no patients around. But somehow, today, with him telling me all of this personal stuff, I thought the name thing was especially odd.

There was more—much more. Dr. Tulip had called her own mother to come bail her out, and when she was released, she swore out a warrant for Dr. Jacobs' arrest. She said he had abused her. Two cops came to the door, handcuffed him and arrested him. This was in front of the boys and his mother. Dr. Jacobs spent the night in jail. He was released the next morning, but he was in a lot of trouble. There was a pending charge of spousal abuse hanging over him. Dr. Tulip and the boys were in Teaneck. She was facing DWI charges. So, both of them had been arrested that weekend. How much more dysfunctional could things have gotten? I could not believe the total mess they had created for themselves.

Dr. Jacobs looked terrible. He was unshaven and unkempt. He told me he had already cancelled the morning patients, but that I should cancel all of the afternoon patients and then go home. He would pay me for the day. I did what I was told. I went home, my head reeling from everything I'd heard that morning. I called Bill and told him the situation. "Wow," he said. "Please tell me you're not going back." Bill did not deserve it, but it was the last straw for the day. I screamed at him.

"Please don't tell me what to do as far as my job is concerned! I've really had just about all the aggravation I can take for one day."

"Lily, calm down," Bill said. "Can you just look at what those crazy people are doing to you?"

"I guess so," I answered. "But at least for now, I'll just see what happens." Later that day, I called my friend Marcie and told her everything.

"Start looking for another job," she advised. "These people are beyond crazy." Marcie and Bill didn't know how right they were, but I went back the next day.

Dr. Jacobs told me to go through the appointment book for the next several weeks and put all of Dr. Tulip's appointments in his time slots. I didn't like that. I felt terrible doing it. He said if any patients asked, to tell them she was unavailable. He only had a few patients that day. When he was not in the operatory with them, he was at my desk ranting and raving about what a bitch Dr. Tulip was and how he would never forgive her for having him arrested. At one point, he actually said, "What good is she, anyway, except for sex, and even that isn't very good."

That did it for me. I decided to leave. I couldn't work in that office anymore. Bill and Marcie had been right. I told Dr. Jacobs that conditions were intolerable, and I needed to leave. "What!" he screamed. "Now she's responsible for my losing my front-desk person! NO! NO! NO! You are not leaving!" At that point, I was really disturbed. I had been listening to him yak about everything and anything for the last two years. This was just too much for me to take.

"I'm leaving," I answered, "and I want a letter of recommendation."

"NO!" he shouted. "I'm not giving you that so you can leave here. It looks bad enough to the patients that she's gone. If you leave, it will look really terrible." At that point I was way beyond annoyed.

"Let's put it this way," I said. "If I don't get my letter of recommendation, then I'm out of here right now. If I get it, then I will stay for three weeks and help you get the office in order."

"Whatever," he answered, defeated. "You write it and I'll sign it." I was proud of myself for standing up to him. I typed a glowing letter of recommendation for myself and he signed it. At least I had that. I would need it.

It was almost an unbearable three weeks, but I had agreed to stay that long. I needed to constantly explain to patients that Dr. Tulip was unavailable. I tried to remain professional and not let the patients know what was going on. It turned out not to matter, because Dr. Jacobs had gone totally nuts and was telling everything to everybody.

Anyone with ears got the honor of listening to Dr. Jacobs. All professionalism was gone. From my front desk, I could hear everything that was being said in his operatory. He was totally out of control. He tried to use every patient as his personal therapist. I was horrified to hear him tell patients his wife was a drunk, that she'd had him arrested out of spite, and her dental work was not good.

Patients would roll their eyes at me as they checked out at the front desk. My interpretation was that they were saying, "Let me out of here." I tried to talk to Dr. Jacobs. I told him how horrible it was to be telling all of his personal problems to patients. He agreed, but he kept on doing just that. When he wasn't telling patients all kinds of inappropriate things, he was talking my ear off. "You know I took on all of her student loans," he complained. "I rolled them over into our mortgage. So, I'm not going to pay her anything, because I'm already paying her bills." I would just look at him and count the days until I could leave. He told me she was not allowed to call the office, and I was to tell him if she did. Right after he gave me those instructions, she called.

"He isn't giving me any money. I have no access to funds. Everything is in his name. See if you can talk to him." It was interesting how Dr. Tulip was suddenly chummy with me, and she was asking for my help. I didn't understand what their financial situation or agreement was, and I certainly did not care. Anyway, I lied to Dr. Jacobs when he asked me if she had called. I was sinking deeper and deeper into the mud hole those two had dug for themselves as well as for those around them.

It was getting extremely nasty at the office. Patients were leaving the practice. We had large blocks of time when there were no patients, and I was forced to listen to Dr. Jacobs rant and rave. He was dealing with his arrest for spousal abuse, and he was ordered to go into an abuser's program. "I can't believe this," he lamented. "Look what that bitch has done." He was constantly referring to her as "the bitch." He would ramble on and on about how he hadn't touched her and how unfair it was for the police to just assume the allegations of abuse were true, because he was such a large man and she was so small. "I yanked her pony tail just to get her off my mother. The bitch was drunk." He went on endlessly. The only saving grace was I knew I would soon be out of his office and out of the on-going war between the two of them. Years ago, I had seen the movie *The War of the Roses*. It was about a feuding couple that ended up wrecking both their lives. This situation reminded me of that movie. The big difference was this was really happening, and somehow, I seemed to be in the middle of it.

All the while, I was looking for another job. I had plenty of experience. Marcie suggested once more that I open myself up to other possibilities, other than dental offices. Again, I didn't listen.

I had learned so much in the dental field. I actually wanted to stay with what I knew. I answered some ads and went for an interview with a Dr. Herbert. He offered me the job right away. His office looked nice. It was in a low-rise office building about twenty minutes from my house. He told me he had let go of his last front-desk manager and therefore needed someone to start as soon as possible. He participated with insurance plans, so that would be a new experience for me—learning to do the insurance write-offs. He offered me the same money I was getting from Dr. Jacobs, and he seemed nice enough. I told him the date I could start. When I told Dr. Jacobs I had found another job he became visibly upset. "I was hoping you would change your mind and stay. I blame that bitch for making you quit." Dr. Jacobs definitely did not understand the situation. I couldn't wait to leave. I walked out of that office at the end of the week, convinced I would never set foot in there again.

THE OTHERS

Chapter 8

I was totally thrilled to be out of the office of Jacobs and Tulip. It had become terribly unpleasant there, and I was happy to no longer be a part of it. Even though Dr. Jacobs gave me a hard time about leaving, he said I was welcome to come back whenever I wanted. *Fat chance,* I thought. *I'm NEVER going back to that loony place again.*

I arrived at Dr. Herbert's office on a day the office was closed. That was planned, so he could go over things with me—especially the way his office dealt with insurance plans.

His office participated in every PPO plan there was. Being a participating provider meant he was contracted to take write offs. The insurance company decided what they would be willing to pay for every procedure. This was called the *allowable amount.* The doctor could charge whatever he wanted, but the insurance company would disallow anything over what they considered to be usual and customary. The doctor would write-off the difference. It was a financial advantage to the patient. It would benefit the doctor, because the insurance company would list him as a participating provider, and the office would acquire more patients.

More patients, however, meant shorter appointment times. There was no extra time built in for socializing or getting to know the patient. It was all business. In order for the practice to make money, patients were given a set amount of time, and the schedule was strictly adhered to. Fillings were scheduled for twenty, thirty, or forty minutes, depending on how many surfaces needed to be filled. Crowns had to be done in an hour, and cleaning appointments could take no longer than forty minutes.

Dr. Herbert used a different computer program than the one I was used to. This one was called Working Dental, and I didn't like it. It wouldn't let me correct the same mistake twice, and this was a problem for me. It had all kinds of controls built into the program. Also, taking payments from patients was done inside the computer program, rather than by a separate charge machine. Of course, Dr. Herbert did not mention that, at least half of the time, the charges didn't go through properly and had to be corrected. That was only part of the stress I would eventually come to experience in my new office.

Dr. Herbert was all business. I wondered to myself if this man ever smiled. He told me he let go of his last two front-desk managers. He said there was a backlog of nine months worth of insurance claims that were processed improperly and they would have to be redone. *Nine months of back insurance claims*! I was totally shocked. In

Dr. Jacobs' office, all claims were sent out the day the service was performed, and if we didn't hear back from the insurance company within three weeks, I would find out what the problem was and work to correct it immediately. How did he expect me to handle nine months of claims that were done incorrectly? Since the computer wouldn't let me correct mistakes that someone had already tried to correct, I knew I would be in for a difficult time. Of course, I didn't realize exactly how difficult it would be.

Even though I was extremely apprehensive, I went home that night, ready to start my new job the following Monday. I was a little troubled that Dr. Herbert had not told me about the backed up claims before I accepted the job. Nevertheless, I was optimistic. I was even looking forward to my new adventure.

It is a huge understatement to say the first week at Dr. Herbert's office was hectic.

He had four computers. It was my job to open the office, turn on all the lights and computers, and make sure everything was ready for the first patient. Also, I needed to check the messages first thing in the morning. I never dreamed there could be so many messages when the day had just begun.

Unlike Dr. Jacobs' office, there was no one there to help me ease into the job. I felt as though I had been thrown into the lion's den. The phone was ringing nonstop, and the fax machine was going constantly. I was checking patients in and out at a furious rate, and I was so busy, I was afraid if I took my hour for lunch, I would get further and further behind.

The backlog of claims was impossible. Since the computer wouldn't let me correct past mistakes that had already been tampered with, I started submitting the old claims like they did in the pre-computer age. This meant getting out old paper forms and doing hours of laborious work by hand.

Dr. Herbert was a nervous wreck. As soon as he was finished with a patient, he would drop that patient's chart on my desk, head for the little closet he used as an office, and slam the door shut. I often wondered what he was doing in there. I had questions about billing the procedures he had just done. I needed to speak with him. He was always unavailable. The few times I knocked on his office door to ask him a question, he would yell, "WHAT?" I was actually afraid of this little man with the nervous disposition. My mind constantly wandered back to Dr. Jacobs' office. Aside from the craziness between the two docs, I had actually enjoyed that job. I was not enjoying this one. I didn't even have time to be friendly to the patients. I was so involved in trying to keep up my pace that I actually felt annoyed when a patient just wanted to talk. I was very troubled by this. In my previous office, I always had time to socialize with the patients and make them feel at ease.

Dr. Herbert could not keep employees around. Unlike Dr. Jacobs and Tulip, who did their own cleanings, most dentists had a regular hygienist and sometimes a dental assistant. Dr. Herbert used a dental agency called Dental Help Associates. Almost every day there was a different hygienist or a different assistant. Sometimes, they would stay for two or three days, but invariably, Dr. Herbert would yell at them or insult them in some way, and they would be gone. I was constantly calling the agency to tell them to send us someone else. On one occasion, Dr. Herbert did not like the way the assistant was holding a piece of equipment. He yanked it out of her hand and gave it to the patient, all the while yelling, "You're not doing that right. The patient could do a better job!" The assistant was mortified. She walked right out. This happened at three o'clock in the afternoon, and we couldn't get a replacement so late in the day. I was forced to cancel the patients for the rest of the day, because Dr. Herbert could not function without an assistant.

Dr. Herbert was so desperate one time he actually called me in to help with a crown. The temporary assistant had not shown up that day, and we were unsuccessful in trying to locate another one. He showed me on the spot how to mix the preparation for an impression. I did the best I could, but I kept wondering what the patient would think if they knew I was totally untrained for dental assisting. Some offices combine the job of front desk with assisting, but none of the offices I had been in did this, so I was totally unprepared. I questioned whether or not the whole scenario was ethical.

I also questioned Dr. Herbert's skill. One patient who came in for a crown really got a shock, when Dr. Herbert told him he did the wrong tooth. The correct tooth still needed to be done, so the patient was required to sit through two crown procedures instead of one. Dr. Herbert told me to only charge him for one. Was he crazy? I thought so. He shouldn't have charged the man for either one of them. But he did, and that patient never came back.

Each night, I would go home exhausted and frustrated. I didn't want to be working in that office. I didn't know what to do. Bill told me to look for something else. I was afraid. I didn't like the idea of job-hopping. I told myself I would give it a little more time. I also thought a lot about

Marcie's warnings. She really believed that all dentists had something weird about them. I never wanted to stereotype like that, but I was beginning to wonder about it. Certainly, in the other dental offices I had worked at, I had witnessed some unsavory practices, as well as some unusual personality issues. Were they all nuts? Did the dental work itself make them crazy? I didn't want to believe that. Surely, I had just encountered some unusual situations.

Conditions started to become unbearable. Every day was a struggle to keep up with the workload. The front desk really could have used a second or even a third person, but there was just me, doing everything. I felt frantic all day long. If I tried to ask Dr. Herbert a question, he usually yelled at me and told me to handle it myself. Some things needed to be handled by the dentist, not me. Sometimes, the insurance company would send a claim back, asking for an explanation from the doctor. When I would ask him about it, he would shrug it off and tell me to take care of it. It was *his* name on the door, not mine. I was getting more and more dissatisfied. Eventually, I couldn't take it any longer. By the time I had been there almost six months, I was getting more and more despondent. In addition, I was getting frequent headaches. I attributed this to stress. I started checking the ads for other jobs.

I talked to Marcie about this a lot. She kept encouraging me to look for a different type of work. I was lost. I didn't know what else I wanted to do, and again, I was so well trained in the dental field that I didn't want to change. I had several interviews planned—all with dental offices. Marcie said, "You know, you're beginning to be a dental whore." We both had a good laugh, but maybe she was on to something.

I felt that I couldn't stay at Dr. Herbert's office any longer. I had interviews planned, and I was confident I would find something else. So, after six months of dental office hell, I handed him a letter of resignation.

I left it on his desk before he arrived:

Dear Dr. Herbert,

This is my letter of resignation. I will stay this week and next week, unless you decide you do not want me here. I have given great effort and attention to this job. I take my responsibilities very seriously and I really did want to make this work. Unfortunately, I feel that whatever I do is never enough and usually, by the end of the day, when we are both very tired, things go from bad to worse. I cannot work in an environment where I am afraid to ask a question and usually the only comments about my work are negative.

I feel I have given one hundred percent to this job. I have worked diligently to help clear your insurance claims. I have been very good with the patients, and I have been able to multi-task more than I ever thought possible. All of this seems not to be enough. This is the only job in my entire life where I am so stressed that I am actually experiencing physical symptoms.

Dr. Herbert, I hope you find what you are looking for in a front-desk manager. I wish you and your practice much success.

Sincerely,
Lily Morgan

Just putting all of that in writing was enough to make me feel vindicated. The job had been pure hell. As I was writing the resignation letter, a wave of relief washed over me. I would soon be away from this situation.

When Dr. Herbert came in that morning, as usual, he went right into his little closet-like office. He came out a few minutes later and said. "Well, Lily, I wish I had done things differently with you. Do you think you could give me three weeks?"

This man has got to be kidding, I thought. So, I lied. "Sorry, I start my new job in two weeks."

It turned out not to be such a lie. I actually did find another job very quickly. I tried to shake off Marcie's comments about my being a *dental whore.* I was ready to begin my new adventure at Delightful Dental Spa.

Chapter 9

Delightful Dental Spa was located in the parking garage of a beautiful luxury high-rise apartment building. Yes, I did say "*in* the parking garage." When I pulled into the lower level of the garage and parked my car, I walked right over to the double glass doors leading into the dental spa.

When I had interviewed with Dr. Hillary Fox, she explained to me how she and her dental partner, Dr. Melanie Marshall, had created Delightful Dental Spa as a relaxing retreat to have dental work done in a soothing, holistic environment. The staff included two hygienists and two dental assistants, as well as a massage therapist, an acupuncturist, and a skin-care specialist. There were plans in the works to eventually include a manicurist.

The waiting area was tastefully decorated in contemporary furniture. There were black leather sofas, glass tables, and a service area offering bottled water and caffeine-free tea. The whole area was lit with softly glowing candles. Soothing, classical music was playing in the background.

Dr. Fox told me they did a lot of cosmetic dentistry. In addition, a patient could come to Delightful Dental Spa, not only to have the look of their smile improved, but also to have a relaxing day of massages, acupuncture, facials, and makeup lessons. Skin care was promoted on the same level as the dental care, and the spa sold a lot of skin-care products.

I arrived at my new job the first day with high aspirations. I was intrigued by the whole idea. I thought this would be a really interesting job. I would be working in the world of beauty, as well as the world of dentistry. They used the same computer program Dr. Jacobs had used, so I didn't have my usual computer fears.

Everything in my new office was geared to selling spa services. When a patient made an appointment to get his or her teeth cleaned, I was required to offer the patient a free mini facial. This was a way of getting them interested in the cosmetic services we offered. During the mini facial, the cosmetician would analyze patients' skin and tell them which products they should buy. Almost every patient who came for the mini facial ended up not only booking a full facial, but also buying the products that had been recommended to him or her. Although we booked more women patients for these services, men loved it, too, and we had several male clients.

I was continually amazed at the amount of money people were willing to spend for their appearance. Many clients would spend a thousand dollars on skin-care products, even after spending many thousands of dollars on veneers for their teeth. Traditional dental services were still offered, but the cosmetic aspects and the skin care reigned supreme.

I was quite busy. I was already good at the dental parts of my job. I had no problem with the dental codes and the insurance. I had plenty of experience in that department. However, I found myself uncomfortable with pushing the skin-care products. I thought they were over-priced, and the practical side of me could not imagine how a two-hundred-dollar face cream could be worth the price. I had always taken care of my skin, and over the years, I received my share of compliments. I always used moisturizers and the like, but I couldn't conceive of people paying exorbitant prices for these products.

The cosmetic dentistry was a different story. Veneers could really improve a person's appearance. A beautiful smile is priceless, although I did feel Delightful Dental Spa over did it in recommending some of these procedures.

Other procedures, like teeth whitening, were also extensively promoted. In many cases, this is a procedure that can really improve a patient's appearance. However, it seemed to me that the two dentists routinely recommended this procedure for almost everyone. Also, it really bothered me that, after the one-hour, chair-side whitening procedure, most patients needed pain killers. I didn't think the procedure was being properly supervised. The weeks went by, and I became increasingly dissatisfied with my working conditions. I told myself I could *not* change jobs again, and I would get used to the parts of my job that made me uncomfortable. Again, my thoughts kept going back to my old job at Dr. Jacobs' office. What was it about that office that made me think about it so much?

The waiting area at Delightful Dental Spa was rather dark. Most of the light in the reception area came from candles, and so much of that dim candlelight was hard on my eyes. The actual lights were kept at a minimum to create *atmosphere*. The worst, however, was looking out on the parking garage. The big double-glass doors were there, but all I could see beyond them was parked cars in a dark garage.

The policy of the office was to work through an eight-hour day. The other offices I had worked at, all had a nine-hour day, with one hour being unpaid for lunch. The dental spa was different. Whenever there was a quiet moment, we could go into the employee lounge and grab a quick bite. No one ever took more than ten minutes for that. So, I was basically in the dark the entire day. It could be a beautiful, sunny day outside, and I would never know it. I would drive into the dark parking garage at 9:00 a.m. and out again at 5:00 p.m. I really missed seeing the sun during the workday. It took me a while to realize this situation was affecting my mood. I was continually tense and felt sapped of energy.

What really made me realize, however, that I had a serious problem with the job, was the lunch policy. It wasn't just that we were required to eat fast. It was the policy that told us *what* we could eat. There were to be no hot meals prepared in the microwave. I couldn't believe it! There was a microwave in the employee lounge, but we were not supposed to use it. Dr. Fox said she didn't want microwave smells interfering with the ambiance of the office. We all thought this was a joke at first, but Dr. Fox was totally serious. So it was cold food only. Anything that could possibly have an odor was banished.

"So," Kimmie said to me when I talked to her by phone one night, "let me get this straight. You have to eat in ten minutes, and you have to bring cold food with no odors." "Unfortunately, that's it," I said. "You know, Mom, it sounds more like a prison than a job." I thought about this. Kimmie was right. I wrote down all the reasons I could think of for not liking to work at Delightful Dental Spa.

I don't get to see the sun.

I have to push products I don't believe in.

I have to gulp down cold food in a hurry.

It's so dark in the reception area that I am straining my eyes.

After I had written all of that, I started to think about my old office of Jacobs and Tulip. I started to feel a little homesick for that office, but I knew there was no going back. I wrote down what I knew in my heart to be true about the office of Dr. Jacobs and Dr. Tulip:

I had a big window, where I could see the sun.

I didn't have to push products.

I could go home for lunch, thereby breaking up the monotony of the day, and I could eat whatever I wanted.

Anyway, I had no intentions of going back to the office of Jacobs and Tulip, but I also came to a decision. I was not happy at Delightful Dental Spa.

I did a fair amount of soul searching. Was it somehow my fault that I was unhappy at all of these jobs? Was it just a matter of rotten luck? Was it just dental offices that came with differing degrees of craziness? I didn't know. I only knew that I could not stay at Delightful Dental Spa.

I handed in my resignation, giving Dr. Fox two weeks notice. Again, I didn't know where I would go next. I had been there five months, and I knew I could not stay. I did feel really bad, not because I was leaving there, but because I was rather disappointed in myself. I was job-hopping again. What was wrong with me? Why was I so unhappy with my last two jobs? I reminded myself how I was happy at the office of Jacobs and Tulip, but quit because of their fighting. It became much too unpleasant for me to stay. I knew this was true, but I still felt like a loser for quitting yet another job.

Talking to Marcie that night she said, "No, you are not a loser, but you are a *dental whore!*" She continued, "Please find something else to do. This dental thing is not working for you."

Oh, Marcie, if only I had listened to you. Again I found myself looking for a job, and the only ads that looked appealing were for dental offices. I told myself I was already trained. I had valuable skills, and nothing else I saw would pay me what I had been getting in the dental offices. So I went on some interviews, and surprise, surprise, I found a job with a very nice dentist named Dr. Donald Depore. He had offices in Livingston and Verona. He wanted me to work in the Verona office. I was sure this time would be the lucky charm. I had high hopes for this job, and the adventure was about to continue.

Chapter 10

I was delighted to be back at a conventional type of dental office. Dr. Depore's Verona office was a small practice, and I was comfortable there. His wife, Sara, was the office manager. She was a rather mousey looking woman, with graying brown hair. She wore no make-up. She was very thin, but not especially fit looking. She dressed to blend into the wallpaper. The contrast between the doctor and his wife was remarkable, because he was a very trim, fit, athletic-looking man. Every day he wore a nice shirt and tie under his lab coat. He had a distinguished looking mustache, and one could tell he cared about his appearance. Dr. Depore was in his fifties, and he was clearly the type of man who commanded a second look from women. He and his wife actually worked well together. He did all the dental work, and she took complete charge of running the office. At the Livingston office, he had an office manager, but his wife Sara was clearly in charge of the Verona office. I was to be the front-desk manager. My duties would be to deal with the patients, and Sara would be behind the scene, in a back office, doing all kinds of administrative work.

I soon learned it was really me who was running the office and Sara was in the back room taking care of personal business, such as talking to her housekeeper, talking to her children who were away at college, and keeping in touch with her aging parents who lived in South Carolina.

The office seemed normal enough. I didn't quite understand why they used dental assistants from Dental Help Associates. In Dr. Herbert's case, I had known why. He was impossible to work with. But Dr. Depore and his wife seemed nice enough. I wasn't sure why they didn't have a regular assistant and hygienist, but every week, the agency would send us two people. Sometimes, we would have the same assistant two or three weeks in a row. The practice only needed a hygienist twice a week, so it was usually a different person on Tuesday and then someone else on Thursday. I wasn't sure what the situation was at his other office, but I imagined it was about the same. He split his time between the two offices, so he was always busy.

At lunch, I always got to talk with the assistants from the agency. They usually didn't have anything bad to say about working there, except that Dr. Depore was really slow and took a very long time for each procedure. They also mentioned he liked to do most things himself, and they usually ended up just being in the operatory with him and the patients, instead of actually helping with the procedures. A couple of the temps also mentioned how good-looking Dr. Depore was. They also said he had a way of looking at them that made them feel like he could see right through their clothes. I never felt that way about him. I agreed he was nice-looking. I thought he didn't look perfectly matched to his wife, but I reminded myself how appearances are often deceiving. Dr. Depore and his wife seemed compatible, at least on the surface. Certainly, there was no open hostility such as what I had witnessed in Dr. Jacobs' and Dr. Tulip's office.

As the weeks wore on, I found some peculiarities with Dr. Depore, but generally things were okay. I noticed he did very few fillings and a lot of crowns. I asked one of the assistants about this. She said she had wondered about that, too. It seemed as though he didn't like to do anything other than a one-surface filling. As soon as there was decay involved in two or three surfaces, he told the patients they needed a crown. Of course, crowns are very expensive. I really did wonder about this, but by that time, I had come to the conclusion that so many dentists are strange and that's just the way things were in the dental world.

It did occur to me that Dr. Depore was taking advantage of patients by recommending services that could have been avoided. However, his patients did seem happy with him. Some of them had been coming to his practice for twenty years or more. So I decided the job was good enough, and I was not up for switching again. At least that's what I told myself.

I had been at Dr. Depore's office several weeks, and I was getting used to seeing a new hygienist sent from the agency every week or so. However, I was not prepared for the last one the agency sent. I could hardly believe my eyes when Dr. Babette Tulip walked in one Tuesday morning. "Lily!" she wailed, "I'm so happy to see you!"

"Dr. Tulip," I responded, somewhat taken aback. "What are you doing here?"

"Well, Lily, I've been doing hygiene through the agency, since Dr. Jacobs and I had that silly separation. Sometimes

I come in as the temporary hygienist, and sometimes I temp as a dentist in various offices."

I was totally surprised. First of all, she was friendlier to me than she ever had been, and second, I never expected to see her doing temp work for an agency. But there was more.

"Dr. Jacobs and I are back together," she said.

"You are?" I managed to inquire.

"Yes," she said. "We worked it out, but we were advised not to work together, so I'm working for the temp agency two days a week, and I'm only back in our regular office two, sometimes three, days a week."

I could hardly believe what I was hearing. *They were back together*! I could only imagine whose insane idea that was. Before I left their office, they had each had the other arrested and were ferociously fighting with one another. I left because it was intolerably nasty and crazy there.

Dr. Tulip continued. "I want to thank you, Lily, for quitting when you did." Obviously, Dr. Tulip thought that by quitting, I had taken her side. Actually, I quit because I could not stand the ugliness that was going on. I had always been more sympathetic to Dr. Jacobs than to Dr. Tulip.

Dr. Tulip seemed to have toned down her image quite a bit. She wore less make-up, and she was actually wearing scrubs, not some weird outfit covered up by a lab coat. She was all sweetness and nice and seemed genuinely happy to see me.

Dr. Depore and his wife really liked her. They told me to call Dental Help Associates and arrange for Dr. Tulip to be at Dr. Depore's office every Tuesday. I kept thinking how strange the whole situation was—my ending up working in the same office as Dr. Tulip. Even stranger was that Dr. Tulip and Dr. Jacobs were back together. It was difficult to run that one through my mind.

And so it continued, me seeing Dr. Tulip every Tuesday at Dr. Depore's office. A few times, I thought I saw some "knowing" glances between Dr. Tulip and Dr. Depore. It seemed that, when Dr. Tulip was near him, Dr. Depore was all smiles, and sometimes, I thought that several of his comments to her were a little too personal. He often told her that she did good work. It wasn't what he said—it was the *way* he said it. I told myself it was my imagination. The job continued to be good enough for me, so I had no intentions of going anywhere else. Dr. Tulip continued being friendlier and friendlier to me. When I had worked for her and her husband, she could be friendly one day and cold the next. But at Dr. Depore's office, she was super friendly all of the time.

Sometimes, when I talked to Dr. Tulip, I felt a little nostalgic for the way things used to be—before Dr. Tulip and Dr. Jacobs went nuts. In the early days, when I worked for them, I was very content. There was always tension between them, but I still considered it to be one of the best jobs I'd ever held. Certainly, it was the most convenient. I lived such a short distance from their office. It was such a small office, and I got to know all of the patients really well. I missed that. I wondered how the two of them were getting along in their office on the days when Dr. Tulip was back working there, and not at Dr. Depore's office.

I brought the subject up with Bill. "You know, Bill, Dr. Depore's office is fine, but seeing Dr. Tulip there so often, sometimes makes me nostalgic for working with Jacobs and Tulip."

"Lily, you need to stop right there." Bill looked a little annoyed. "We've been through this many times. Those people were more than crazy. Why would you even *think* of going to work for them again?"

"I know you're right, Bill. It's just that I really miss the patients there. I think the good really outweighed the bad," I added. "They're back together again. She's only in the office with him three days a week. How bad can it be?"

Bill let out a long sigh, which sounded a little like a moan. "Look, Lily, I know you will do what you want, anyway, but I really believe it would be a big mistake for you to work for them again. Besides, they haven't even asked you to come back."

That situation was about to change. On my way home one evening, I got the call on my cell phone. It was Dr. Tulip. "Lily," she said, sounding as sweet as possible, "Dr. Jacobs would really like it if you would come and talk to him."

"Why?" I asked.

"He really hasn't been happy since you left. Mary, who replaced you, can now only give us part time hours, and he really wants you back." I wasn't quite sure what to say, and I didn't know why she, instead of Dr. Jacobs, was calling me, but I agreed to go over there the following evening and meet with Dr. Jacobs. Part of me was really interested in going back to work for them. I hadn't realized how much I missed their office. None of the other ones, certainly not the first two, were even remotely as enjoyable to work in. Dr. Depore's office was okay, but I still had derived more satisfaction from working in Dr. Jacobs' office.

I talked to Bill about it that night. Dear, sweet, wonderful Bill. He told me once again how he thought it was a mistake for me to return to the office of Jacobs and Tulip. "Do you remember all the tension between the two of them?" he asked. "Do you remember what happened that Thanksgiving weekend?"

"Of course I remember, but I'm willing to give it another chance. I feel like I have to at least try."

"Okay, do what makes you happy."

"You make me happy, Bill." My husband gave me one of his famous grins and said, "Well, I guess you're going back."

I met with Dr. Jacobs the following evening. He really wanted me to come back to work for him. "We worked well together, didn't we Lily?"

"Yes, we did," I said. "But all that messy, nasty stuff—is that over with?"

"I hope so," he said. He didn't say much else about his personal life but started to talk about some of the changes that had been made inside the office since I had been gone. We no longer used an appointment book, along with the computer software; we now just relied on the computer program alone. Some of the office procedures had been streamlined, such as only putting financial information for patients in the computer instead of putting it in the individual patient charts. All of this was fine with me. I told Dr. Jacobs I needed to give Dr. Depore at least two weeks notice, and then I would begin. He was agreeable to that.

Dr. Depore and his wife Sara were not happy. They didn't think it was fair that Dr. Tulip and Dr. Jacobs were taking me back. It seemed to ruin the relationship between Dr. Tulip and the two of them, and they wanted the agency to send a different hygienist. Nevertheless, they asked if I could stay at least three weeks. I told them I would only stay two weeks. This further aggravated the situation, and it was a little strained for the next two weeks. Nevertheless, it worked out, and Dr. Depore and Sara started interviewing for my replacement. They actually found someone who was ready to start when my two weeks were done.

"Here you go, again, Lily. The dental whore continues," Marcie chided.

"It will work out, Marcie, you'll see," I tried to reassure her. "I really do want to go back to Dr. Jacobs' office."

"Did you forget how crazy that office was?" she asked.

"No. I didn't forget. I know things there got dicey, but I really do want to go back. Be happy for me."

"OK," she said. "Don't say I didn't warn you."

That night, I thought about all the previous dental offices where I had worked. I had to admit to myself they were all strange. I wondered if all dentists were a little bit off in the mental department. There was that first dentist I had worked for several years before. He made racial slurs about patients and was a total bigot. Then there was Dr. Jacobs and Dr. Tulip. For sure, those two were highly unconventional, but I still liked working there. Dr. Herbert was really awful to work for. I never did know what he did all those times he ran into his little closet-like office and slammed the door. He was totally disorganized, and he rushed through procedures and made huge mistakes. In addition, he often took his frustrations out on me. Then there was Delightful Dental Spa. The two dentists there seemed to put most of their focus on lavish spa services, instead of dental services. Finally, in Dr. Depore's office, fillings almost always became crowns. I really think he did some unnecessary procedures. I wondered, *Are all dentist nuts? Have they all gone mental?* I corrected my thoughts. *Perhaps they've GONE DENTAL.* I laughed to myself with that thought, and then I gratefully went to sleep.

TOGETHER AGAIN

Chapter 11

I was incredibly relieved to be back at my old office. I had not realized just how comfortable I was when I worked at the office of Jacobs and Tulip. Yes, I left because it had become contentious and mean between the two docs, but in comparison with working at Dr. Herbert's office, Delightful Dental Spa, and Dr. Depore's office, I felt like I was back where I belonged.

I loved seeing all the old patients. They, in turn, were happy to see me. Frequently, when I would answer the phone, I would get, "Lily, is that you? When did you get back?" It made me feel terrific. This office was so unhurried compared with Dr. Herbert's office and I didn't miss the pressure I was under to sell products at Delightful Dental Spa. I truly believed things had worked out, and this could actually be the last job I would ever have.

Dr. Tulip was only working in our office two or three days a week. The other days, she was still taking jobs from the agency. (Of course, she was no longer taking any jobs in Dr. Depore's office.) I hadn't asked Dr. Jacobs anything about what had transpired between him and Dr. Tulip in the year and a half I had been away. I naturally assumed they had worked out their differences. After all, they were back together, weren't they? I could not have been more mistaken.

It wasn't long before Dr. Jacobs was back to his old habit of yakking at my desk whenever he had a free moment. I wasn't back even a week, when he started complaining about his wife. As usual, I didn't have to say anything. Dr. Jacobs could talk endlessly, whether or not I would stop what I was doing and listen to him. He just kept on talking. Sometimes, I would barely look at him, but at other times, I couldn't help myself, and I would actually become interested and take part in the conversation.

"You know, Lily, I only agreed to get back together with her because she accepted a job in upstate New York."

"What do you mean? She's here. What's all this about New York?"

"Well," he continued, "we were in the middle of pursuing a divorce. She was threatening all sorts of things. It was going to be extremely nasty and bitter. All of our papers were drawn up. I was going to have to fight her for my right to get visitation with my kids. All of the abuse charges she filed against me had been dropped. There never was any case. But everything else was up for grabs. You know the house and practice have always been in my name, but she was still going after the jugular."

Again I took the bait. "What do you mean? How could everything have been in your name only?"

"When we bought the practice, which is in the house, we put it all in my name, because she has lousy credit," he explained. I was shocked at this. I wondered how any woman, but especially one who was so educated, could let herself be put in that position. He continued. "I took on all her student loans. I paid all the bills. I work my ass off in this practice, and all she does is sit on hers. I rolled the mortgage and the student loans into one big refinance and, now, my mortgage is about the same as the value of the house. So she can have the house, because half of nothing is nothing." I was trying to keep up with him as he kept rambling. "But the practice is another story. You know she hardly works here. You've seen it. If I lose the practice, I have nothing. That bitch was trying to say half of it should be hers."

"All right," I said, "but what does any of this have to do with New York?"

"Well," he continued, "she was working for that damn agency as a hygienist, and I guess she was sending out resumes, and she got an offer to work as a dentist in upstate New York. She came to me and said we should end all of this craziness, get back together for the kids. She said she would work in New York during the week and only come back here on weekends. All I could think of was that I could have my kids and not have to lose my practice if the judge decided against me."

"So you reconciled because you didn't want to face what might have happened in court, and you thought she would be gone during the week, anyway?"

"You got it," he said.

"So what happened to the job in New York?"

"The bitch got fired! I should have known. She can't take orders from anyone. Everything has to be her way. Apparently, she was extremely disrespectful to the front-desk person, and the dentist fired her. You know, Lily, it's harder to find a good front-desk person than some piss-assed junior dentist to work in a practice."

I didn't quite know what to make of all this. I knew I should stay completely out of it. But it was really hard. I had recently just returned to the practice. I thought things between Dr. Jacobs and Dr. Tulip had calmed down. I was completely wrong about that. He was telling me he really did want a divorce, but they had reconciled under false pretenses. Now they were back in the same house, working at least two or three days a week together. He told me the therapist had warned them not to work together, but they were doing it anyway—at least for those two or three days a week.

This all sounded to me like a terrible situation. How in the world was this arrangement going to work? I also was concerned about Dr. Jacobs' emotional state. He was extremely nervous. His language had deteriorated to a new low. He used profanity all the time. He constantly referred to his wife as "the bitch." I could not believe I was back in this situation. I didn't want to leave again. I did not see that as a viable option. I just couldn't see myself searching for yet another job. So I chose to stay and do the best I could. I would be pleasant to both of them but try not to get too involved. At least, that was my plan.

Bill wasn't buying it. "What do you mean you won't get involved this time? Lily, I'm telling you now. Going back was a mistake. It's not too late. Just tell them you didn't think it through and you're not staying. You can take your time to find another job. It doesn't have to be in a dental office. You've had no luck there."

I didn't want to listen. For me, there was a definite pull towards staying connected with Drs. Jacobs and Tulip. "Bill, please try to understand. I'm not ready to quit." I really wanted Bill to see my side of it. "No, Lily, you've got blinders on when it comes to them. They are never going to change, and you'll just be pulled deeper into their messy lives." By that time, I was getting really agitated. It probably was because I knew deep inside that Bill was right. I didn't want to admit it. I knew the office of Jacobs and Tulip was pure trouble, but I needed and wanted to keep working there.

Now that the two docs were back together, there was a frantic attempt to pull in more patients. Dr. Tulip seemed to be in manic mode. She constantly complained how we needed to market the practice more. Dr. Tulip knew nothing about running the practice, so nothing she said made any sense. Dr. Jacobs seemed to be in some kind of defense mode, where he was trying not to argue with his wife. It seemed to me that he was going along with all her ideas just to pacify her. Then, when she went upstairs, he was back at my desk complaining about how irrational and bizarre her behavior was.

The whole situation was beyond crazy. Dr. Tulip started going through all of the archived charts—patients who had not been coming to the practice for years. "Lily, write a letter to these patients. Tell them I am back, and we would welcome them returning to our practice." This was a terrible idea. Dr. Tulip was telling me to write letters to patients who had left several years ago. Of course,

Dr. Jacobs was at my desk complaining about this. "Just do it, Lily. You and I know it doesn't make sense, but I can't argue with her anymore."

So I wrote the letters and not one patient came back. As far as Dr. Jacobs not arguing with his wife, that just didn't happen. What did happen was that every day she would come up with another ridiculous idea, and he would go along with it. Then, they would blame each other when it didn't work, and he would be back to whining at my desk all day.

Their fighting became a constant factor during the day. Every glance, every comment became a source of friction. Often, they wouldn't even wait for patients to leave the office. They would go into the back room to fight, but the patients could almost always hear what was going on. Furthermore, they didn't even make a pretense of hiding their situation from me. Many times, when the waiting room was empty, they would actually stand in front of my desk screaming at each other. Sometimes, I think I became desensitized to what was going on. It sounds strange, but there were times when it just seemed like a normal part of the day.

This state of affairs continued for several weeks. Then, one day, Dr. Jacobs announced to me how he was going to control his temper and try to make things work for the sake of his kids. "I'm on the ten-year plan," he said. "I don't love her, I don't want to be with her, but I need to be here for my kids. When they're in college, I'll leave." None of this made any sense to me. I suspected he was just afraid of the whole process. I thought how he would rather be in a known hell than the unknown hell that would surely erupt if he actually did try to get a divorce.

So life in the office of Dr. Jacobs and Tulip continued. Both of them seemed to be miserable. He was controlling his temper in the office, but he continued to tell me things that I never asked but couldn't stop him from talking about. He complained constantly about her drinking. He told me over and over again that she was an alcoholic, and he was having a harder and harder time putting up with her constant mood changes. According to him, she blamed him for everything. He also said she was threatening him. She kept bringing up the past, especially what had happened that fateful Thanksgiving weekend. She wanted to constantly keep him in line. She kept threatening to go to the dental board and report him for all kinds of misdeeds. Anytime he disagreed with her, she threatened to tell the board he was a wife abuser—that he did terrible dental work and was unfit to keep his license.

All of this seemed terribly absurd. If he really were an abuser, why was she putting up with it? Why was *he* so afraid of *her*? This man seemed genuinely afraid of his wife. He was no prize, but I didn't picture him as the monster she was portraying him to be. Sometimes, too, it was hard to picture her as the totally mentally disturbed person he made her out to be. However, I did see her behavior as erratic and unpredictable. I never realized to what extent, until I saw it for myself, when the postcard incident happened.

Chapter 12

For quite a while now, Dr. Tulip had been telling Dr. Jacobs they needed to advertise the practice. For weeks, I was busy talking to different advertising publications. They would be placing ads for the practice in several places—mostly local community papers and the like. Dr. Jacobs told me they had tried this approach before—prior to when I first came to work for them. He said he didn't believe this approach would actually work, but he was giving in (as usual) to whatever Dr. Tulip wanted him to do.

He was so afraid of Dr. Tulip that, when I talked to him about this, he would reiterate how she was always threatening to call the police and say he was abusing her. If that didn't work, she would go to the dental board. It was very strange. According to him, she would be threatening him one minute and then be "lovey-dovey" the next. I didn't witness that kind of behavior in the office. What I saw was extreme moodiness and pickiness on her part, but not the threats that Dr. Jacobs kept complaining about.

Anyway, Dr. Tulip said we needed to mail out advertising postcards. She actually wanted to do them herself. She found an on-line print company and said she was ordering one thousand cards. She refused to show the proofs to either Dr. Jacobs or to me. He wanted to see them before the final order, but as usual, he didn't stand up to her, and the cards were ordered without anyone, except Dr. Tulip, seeing the proofs.

When I got to work that morning, the cards were on my desk with a note from Dr. Tulip to go ahead and put the mailing labels on them. *Oh, my God,* I thought when I looked at the cards. Experience was spelled wrong. I couldn't believe it. No way could we send out advertising postcards with a misspelling. Just then, Dr. Jacobs appeared. "Look at this." I said.

"Damn it," he said. "How did that happen?" We both knew how it happened—Dr. Tulip, thinking she knew everything and not letting anyone check the proofs.

Dr. Jacobs started back up the stairs and met Dr. Tulip, as she was coming down the stairs. I heard him show her the misspelling and I heard her scream really loudly, "They're fine. Send them out. It doesn't matter!" Then I heard her go back upstairs and slam the door. Dr. Jacobs came back to my desk. "See what I mean, Lily? She can't be wrong about anything. She would rather send these cards out like they are, rather than admit she didn't do a good job of ordering them."

I could not believe how stupid the whole situation was. Of course the cards were not fit to be sent out, and Dr. Jacobs told me not to mail them. "Just put everything on hold. I need to leave for an appointment with my psychologist." He then left.

It couldn't have been more than two minutes later, when I heard Dr. Tulip's footsteps coming down the stairs.

She was livid. She was screaming at me, "You had no business reading those cards! Your job is to do what you are told, and you were told to address the cards, not to read them!" I could not believe what I was hearing. I was stunned, but I tried to stay composed. I was dealing with a lunatic.

"May I say something?" I asked. She had a really wild look in her eyes. I had never before seen her like that.

"NO!" she shouted, and proceeded to turn her back to me and walk away.

I was not to be stopped. "I did nothing wrong," I said. "The word *experience* was spelled wrong, and I needed to tell the both of you."

She looked like a wild woman. "Your job is to do as you are told! You work for me! Watch it! You are on very shaky ground. If you want to continue working here, you do not challenge me! Your job is to do as you are told! You did not pay for the cards! You did not order the cards, and you had no right to read the cards!"

Was she serious? Did she really say I had no right to read the cards? These were advertising postcards. If I had not caught the misspelling, and the cards had gone out, I would have been the first one to be blamed. I sensed I needed to diffuse the situation, so I told her I did not mean any disrespect, but I had done nothing wrong. She got angrier and angrier. Then she said, "And you called upstairs before we had our morning coffee." Now *this* was really ridiculous. Office hours were eight to five. I called upstairs at ten past eight. The woman was out of control. She quickly turned and stomped back upstairs.

I was shaking. How dare she talk to me that way? I now believed every vile thing Dr. Jacobs had ever said about her. He constantly talked about her irrational moods and how she blamed everyone around her for mistakes she herself made. Suddenly, it all made sense to me. She was really a sick woman. Her behavior was far out of the range of normal. Dr. Jacobs had been telling me all along that his wife was an alcoholic. Perhaps she really was. I thought about walking out. I was truly stunned, and didn't know what to do.

Just then, I again heard her footsteps on the stairs. Only about five minutes had passed since her outburst. She was strangely calm. She came over to my desk and, in her sweetest fake voice said, "Can I see the schedule for tomorrow?" Without a word, I pulled up the calendar on the computer screen. She glanced at it and walked away.

Who in their right mind acts that way? I guess that was the point. She was not in her right mind. What should I do? Should I walk out and let her suffer the consequences when she had to explain to Dr. Jacobs where I went? Should I stay? I was pondering all of this, when I heard Dr. Jacobs come home and down the backstairs to the office.

I told him what had happened. He was horrified, but not surprised. "I told you, Lily, this is what she is like. She cannot be wrong about anything." I actually felt sorry for the man. I knew he had a temper. I knew he was prone to bad language, but he always treated me with respect. *Is this what he puts up with on a daily basis?* I actually said to him, "Now I see what you've been talking about all this time. She truly is a bitch."

His response was, "Please, Lily, don't quit."

"Well, today was terrible, but you know I do like this job," I said. "Usually, my interaction is with you, not her.

I'll stay for now, but I have to tell you this. If she *ever* talks to me like that again, I'm out of here."

"I'm really sorry," he said. "But maybe now you'll understand." At that point, I was feeling kind of sorry for him. I actually told him if he ever needed me to testify against her I would.

My saying that was probably a huge mistake. I never thought that everything between them was all Dr. Tulip's fault. However, what just transpired made me feel very sympathetic towards him, and I was not having any kind thoughts about her at all.

Dr. Jacobs seemed to relish my comments. I could tell he was thinking he now had someone on his side. This wasn't quite the case. I still did not want to be in the middle of their marital mess. But I wasn't ready to quit the job, and I now had a clearer insight into what a "head-case" Dr. Tulip was. What I did not see, however, was how I had blinders on when it came to my job. I should have left. But I stayed.

Dr. Jacobs took the whole incident as a sign he could now complain to me about his wife even more than he already did. I didn't mean for that to happen. But it was too late. He lost all sense of decorum. From that point on, he thought he could tell me all sorts of sordid details, whether I was interested or not. His language became worse and worse. He would pepper his comments about his wife with obscenities. I told him I didn't like the language. He would always apologize, but then ten minutes later, he was at it again. Often, while he would have a patient in the chair, he would walk out of the operatory and over to my desk. He would start talking again about whatever injustice

Dr. Tulip had heaped upon him that day. My usual response was, "Don't you have a patient in the chair?"

He would answer back, "It's all right, they're getting numb, and so I have a minute to talk to you."

Why in the world was I staying at this crazy office? I started asking myself that more and more. I really wasn't sure why I stayed. I think I was afraid. I was afraid of leaving and landing in another office I didn't like. Also, if I were really honest with myself, maybe I was getting a little too interested in the daily drama of it all.

Their fights went from bad to worse. Some I witnessed, some I did not. The ones I witnessed were really bad. I could only imagine what the ones I didn't witness were like. Almost every day, he had another war story to complain about. It didn't do any good to ignore him. He was at my desk a good portion of the day. I have to admit, the stories were sometimes interesting. It occurred to me, on several occasions, that maybe I should write a book.

LOTS OF MENTAL,
NOT MUCH DENTAL

Chapter 13

It was eight-fifteen in the morning, and two patients were in the waiting room. It was my usual practice to call upstairs when the first patient arrived. I had placed the call several minutes before, but so far, neither dentist had come downstairs. I always felt bad when patients were kept waiting for an unreasonable length of time. From the waiting room, one could hear sounds coming from the house above the office. It was clear that an argument was taking place upstairs. I was very embarrassed for the patients. I knew they could hear, so I turned up the volume on the office radio. While I couldn't make out the exact words, it sounded really fierce.

Suddenly, the voices got louder, and it was obvious the two docs were coming down the back stairs. He was screaming. "That's it bitch! If you don't see your patient right now, we're finished." Then it was her voice we all heard. "It's *your* practice. You refuse to put my name on it, even though I work like a dog. So, it's *your* problem. I'm not seeing any patients in *your* practice."

Then I heard her footsteps, clomping back up the stairs. I was totally mortified. I went to the back of the office. Dr. Jacobs was standing at the foot of the stairs. His face was red, and he was breathing hard. "That fucking bitch!" He repeated it three times. "She started in on me last night. She kept saying if I wouldn't put her name on the practice, then she wasn't going to see patients. I can't put her name on the practice. If I do, she'll go right to the police, say I abused her, and have me thrown out of the house, so she can have everything. The practice is in the house, and that will be the end of my livelihood. Who the hell does she think pays the bills around here? She only sees about six patients a week in this office."

"Slow down," I pleaded, to no avail. "Why are you so afraid of her? You keep saying she made all of this abuse stuff up. Why are you letting her get to you like this?"

"Listen, Lily, the bitch had me arrested that terrible Thanksgiving. She'll do it again in an instant. She'll make up charges. She won't care if they are true or not."

All of this was going on while there were patients listening in the waiting room. "What do you want me to do?" I asked.

"Cancel all of her patients for today. I think there are just three of them. Make up some excuse and reschedule them to see me, not her, another day."

I sheepishly went back into the waiting room. I told Dr. Tulip's patient we would have to reschedule. The patient couldn't get out of there fast enough. She didn't want to reschedule and she never came back to our office. Dr. Jacobs came out to the waiting room and took the patient who was there to see him. Then he began telling the poor man all sorts of personal stuff he should not have been talking about. I cancelled Dr. Tulip's remaining patients for the day.

I was extremely rattled. I called Bill. "Quit," he said.

"No, I'm not going to do that." I wasn't in the mood for another argument with Bill about this very old subject. I got off the phone quickly. I didn't really understand what exactly was keeping me there. This dental office was truly a toxic, but strangely addicting, place to be. Knowing all of that, maybe I really didn't want to understand.

Dr. Jacobs' patient left, and of course, he was back at my desk. I was disgusted with both dentists. Naturally, he blamed everything on her. "She drank a whole bottle again last night. She was fucking drunk. She screamed in front of the kids how she was going to report me to the dental board. She was going to have my license, and she was going to call the police again."

"I can't listen to any more of this." I had said this many times before, but somehow he always kept talking, and I always seemed to be listening.

"I'm just going to bide my time," he continued, "until I'm in a more stable financial position, and then I'll leave." I didn't believe him at all. I knew they were both miserable. I knew he kept saying she was needling him day and night. I knew this most recent incident would blow over in a few hours or in a few days, and then it would all start up again.

It was a constant pattern with them. There was no end to the supply of issues they fought over. The main one was her unwillingness to do any real work in our office. There were two days every week when she worked away from our office as a hygienist, but lately, she had rarely been available in our practice. Even on the days she was scheduled to be at our office, she would leave the house, and I couldn't schedule any patients for her. They had a weird co-dependent, sick relationship. I felt I was in the middle of a live soap opera.

It got even weirder when Dr. Tulip started talking endlessly about buying her own practice. She really was too stupid to run a practice by herself. She had no business sense whatsoever. She had no knowledge of how insurance worked, and more importantly, she couldn't do even the simplest of dentistry without calling Dr. Jacobs into her room to help her. On the rare occasion when she did do some restorative work, a filling or a crown, she would get halfway through and then find some excuse to get Dr. Jacobs to come and help her. Even I could see she really didn't know much about dentistry. I often wondered how she even made it through dental school. I once asked Dr. Jacobs that question and he said that she had cheated her way through. I didn't know if it were true or not, but I believed she truly must be delusional to think she could run a whole practice. She was a great hygienist. In my opinion, she should have remained a hygienist and never sought to become a dentist.

She wanted Dr. Jacobs to co-sign a loan for her. He wouldn't do it. The arguments that followed were harrowing. Many times, in the middle of the day, they would both go upstairs. I could hear a lot of yelling. We had lost numerous patients, so there was ample opportunity in the day for all of this to transpire. Strangest of all was they could be bitterly fighting one minute and then all was just fine the next. The only constant was him at my desk every chance he got, always pleading his case, always telling me how horrible and wicked she was. Believe me, he was not worth the fight. He had a vile temper, and I had some amount of sympathy for anyone who was married to him. However, I never saw anyone to be such a master at provoking as Dr. Babette Tulip.

Sometimes, a few days would actually go by and things would be quiet. However, this was not the case on one particular morning, when we didn't have any early patients. Since the docs never came downstairs until the first appointment arrived, I decided to organize some files in the back of the office. I hadn't before realized that the back file cabinet was directly under a vent. Not only was Dr. Jacobs' voice coming through, but also it was loud and clear. "You fucking bitch, you fucking bitch!" He said it numerous times. I was really uncomfortable. He was screaming out of control. I could hear her, too, but couldn't make out what she was saying. He, in turn, was using every profanity he knew. It was vile and intense. I was extremely uncomfortable. As I walked back to my desk, I glanced out the window. I saw Justin and Teddy leaving the house for the school bus. So these two messed up adults were arguing in front of those little boys! This was really bad. Justin and Teddy looked forlorn. I felt very sorry for them.

I was truly disgusted with both the docs. How could they put their children through that kind of ugliness? When Dr. Jacobs came down, he started, as usual, to dump his problems on me. "Wait, just a minute," I said. "I could hear you upstairs, and I have to tell you that nothing excuses your using that kind of language to your wife."

Of course he started to explain. "Never mind," I said. "I really don't want to hear it. I saw Justin and Teddy leave for school after all the shouting. What is wrong with you, allowing that to happen in front of the boys?" He looked a little sheepish and then proceeded to tell me how she had provoked him. "You know," I said, "I've always been sympathetic to you because I know how wacky she is and how she wears you down. But I've just witnessed your temper, and I don't like it." He was very apologetic, but somehow things had changed. I saw clearly for the first time how verbally abusive he could be.

The rest of the day was torture. Dr. Tulip came downstairs looking like hell and told me to cancel the rest of her patients for the day. That was always an unpleasant task. I didn't know why they had any patients left.

Later in the day, Dr. Jacobs was back at my desk, talking about what a bitch his wife was.

Then she came home, and he went upstairs to talk to her. Things were calm for the rest of the afternoon, but in the office of Jacobs and Tulip, things never stayed calm for very long.

* * *

I was in the house where I grew up. I don't know how old I was. Maybe I was ten or eleven. We were sitting in the dining room. The dining room table was actually an old kitchen table. It was yellow. My father sat at one end. My mother sat at the other. My sister sat across from me. We could see what was coming. Mom was nagging. I don't know about what. Daddy was getting redder and redder in the face. Why wouldn't she stop provoking him? She kept on and on. She was impossible. My sister and I knew what was coming. We looked at each other. Then, as expected, it happened. Daddy stood up, and slammed his fist on the table. "You goddamned son of a bitch woman! You're no goddamned good! You just keep on and on. You don't know when to stop." Then my mother stood up and began screaming back at him. The yelling was ugly. She was calling him a "failure"— a "nothing." He continued screaming even more profanities at her.

They kept yelling and belittling at each other. My sister and I ran into the bedroom we shared. We got into my bed and pulled the covers over our heads. The screaming was intense. "Make it stop," I pleaded to myself. I was scared. I held on to my sister. Both of us were crying.

* * *

I woke up. Bill was shaking me. "Lily," he said, "You were crying. What's wrong?" "Oh, Bill, I know now why I keep dreaming about the house where I grew up. I also know why I can't seem to leave that lunatic office where I work."

It truly was an enlightening moment for me. I had tried to push away all of those bad childhood memories. The similarities were uncanny. My parents engaged in one vicious argument after the next. Usually, following one of those arguments, my mother would call a taxi. My father would go into their bedroom, mumbling all the time about her being a "bitch, a witch, and a shrew." Then the front door would slam and she was off to her mother's—my grandmother. There she would stay until a week or so later, when my father would beg her to come back, and all would be fine, until the next argument. Sometimes it would be a week. Sometimes it would be a month, but the arguments came on a regular basis. She would frequently leave, he would beg her to come back, and the whole cycle would repeat itself. Each time it happened, I was crushed. I always feared that my mother would not come back. She was hard to live with. She was never happy. She complained all the time. She belittled my sister and me when we weren't the perfect children she thought she deserved to have. She endlessly provoked my father. But she was the only mother I had, and I was afraid of losing her. Interestingly, however, I never blamed my father for any of this.

I had been dreaming about my childhood home for months. Now, it suddenly all made sense. Somehow, the sick situation at the office actually felt familiar. I possessed a new awareness. Dr. Jacobs had a horrible temper, just like my father. Dr. Tulip was the great provoker, just as my mother had been. She was annoying as hell and seemed to almost enjoy seeing how far she could go before her husband lost all control.

Having this awareness didn't really change things much. But I did understand myself a little better. Was I staying at that office to see if I could fix things? I never could fix anything between my parents. I truly felt sorry for Justin and Teddy. I thought I really understood what they were going through, but I wasn't completely sure exactly why I was staying in that situation. Maybe I was staying simply because it was a good job (when they weren't fighting) and maybe I was staying out of curiosity to see what would happen next.

* * *

Chapter 14

Robert and Babette were in the kitchen. It was the weekend—Saturday evening. He was standing in front of the refrigerator, with the door open. As he started to reach for some leftovers, she grabbed his arm. "I bought that food. I paid for it out of my paycheck," she said. "You say the practice is yours—won't put my name on it. If that's the way you want it, fine. Then don't eat the food I buy with the money I earn." Justin and Teddy ran upstairs. They knew not to be in the line of fire when this kind of thing started.

"Listen, Bitch, I support the family," Robert was quick to respond. "Who do you think pays the mortgage, your credit card bills, your car insurance, everything? So you go to the grocery store. So what," he countered. "The only bills you have to pay are the grocery store and the housekeeper." He continued to take food out of the refrigerator.

She went over to him. "Just wait until I see to it that you get yours!" she screamed even louder. "You abused me back at that awful Thanksgiving weekend, and I haven't forgotten it. I can still call the cops on you and tell them you're an abuser. And furthermore, I'm reporting you to the dental board. Your conduct is unbefitting a dentist. I'll tell them about the lousy veneers you put on Michael Lister. Just wait until I get my own practice and write a letter to *your* patients telling them what a scumbag you really are. Your work is lousy. I'll get patients to testify." As she was screaming all of this, she grabbed the plate of food from his hands and threw it into the trash.

"You fucking bitch, I'll show you abuse!" He was out of control and grabbed her around the neck with his left arm and grabbed the sharp kitchen scissors with his right. He held the scissors to her throat. "You fucking *whore*, you fucking *bitch*, I've had enough!" He held her like that for about thirty seconds, and as he released his grip, she ran screaming up the stairs to their bedroom. She locked the door and called 911.

He was standing in the kitchen, shaking. He had completely lost control. He knew better. Had he played right into her hands? Was that what she wanted? Did she try to push him just to see how out of control he would get? He heard the police car pull up to the house. Dr. Tulip ran out to meet them. He, too, came outside. He didn't want whatever was about to happen to be in front of the children.

The police questioned both of them. He was still shaking. Somehow she seemed calm and in control. She told the police it was just a small argument and she did not want to press charges. She did not tell them about the scissors. The police did not file a report.

They didn't talk the rest of the evening. He didn't know what to make of the situation. She woke him up in the middle of the night to have sex. He obliged.

* * *

The following Monday, when I showed up for work, Dr. Jacobs seemed unusually tense and nervous. I made the mistake of asking him if everything was all right. "No," he said, and he told me what had transpired on Saturday night. I was horrified. He told me the whole story—even the sex part, which I did not particularly want to hear.

"You held scissors to her throat?" I could hardly believe what I was hearing.

"I lost control," he said. He looked destroyed. "She wouldn't stop tormenting me. I got so angry, I just blew."

I was very troubled by all of this. "Look," I said. "Nothing, absolutely nothing, can justify your threatening her with a weapon. You need to get out of this marriage, NOW. If you can get that angry, you have to remove yourself from the situation immediately."

"I can't leave now," he pleaded.

Totally puzzled, I asked, "Why not?"

"If I leave now, she'll report me to the police. I called my lawyer. He said I should just calm down emotionally and wait six months. After that amount of time has gone by, she won't be able to have any credibility if she reports me," he continued. "I don't know why, Lily, but she's hanging on to this farce of a marriage for dear life. Now, she'll use the scissors incident to blackmail me into staying."

Did this man have any idea how ridiculous his reasoning sounded? Did his lawyer really think Dr. Jacobs was capable of calming down? "You're just making excuses," I said. "If you're that miserable, you need to get out before you really lose your temper and kill her."

"I wish she were dead," he replied, "but I'm not going to kill her. Maybe she'll just drop dead from all the booze she drinks every night."

Why was I even bothering to reason with this man?

"I'm voluntarily putting myself in an anger management class," he said. "I already enrolled."

"That's good," I answered. "You could really use that. But I still think you need to get out of this marriage now."

"No," he said, "I'm going to my anger management class. I'm seeing my therapist once a week, and after six months, I'll tell her I want a divorce."

I was very frustrated with him. He certainly was an abuser. He admitted to holding a dangerous weapon to his wife's throat—that was totally out of range of being even remotely acceptable. The whole situation was spinning out of control. I was glad he was going to anger management classes, however, and I was glad he was seeing a therapist. But I didn't believe for a minute he could just coast along for another six months. She was an alcoholic. She was endlessly picking at him, chastising him, and belittling him. He had an explosive temper and couldn't be trusted to control himself. What he did was inexcusable. However, she showed no signs of wanting to leave the marriage. For whatever sick reason, she was hanging on to this lethal, poisonous union.

According to Dr. Jacobs, his wife's spending habits, as well as her drinking, were out of control. They were fighting all the time. She often provoked him, just to see how far she could go before he snapped. He claimed he felt awful about the scissors incident and swore to me he would never do anything like that again. I didn't see how anything but a dreadful outcome could be borne from all of this.

I constantly thought about those little boys upstairs. These two crazy dentists were both so narcissistic, so caught up in their own private wants and needs, they either couldn't or *wouldn't* see what damage they were doing to their children. They both considered themselves to be good parents. I guess that didn't include having any respect for the other parent. The children had an alcoholic mother, one who was unpredictable as well as unstable, and they had a father who had a volatile temper and who was physically threatening to their mother.

* * *

Chapter 15

Robert actually believed he could rein in his temper. He was faithfully going to his anger-management class. There was a lot of writing involved. After the leader had spoken on a given topic for the evening, the participants were to write in their personal journals. They were to express their feelings truthfully—talking in their private journals about what made them angry, and how they felt when they expressed that anger.

Robert Jacobs was making a sincere effort. In his journal, he wrote about all of his frustrations. He wrote how he hated his wife. He wrote how she seemed to take joy in provoking his anger, and he wrote how he was disgusted by his own inability to change the situation.

He kept his journal in his car. In the middle of the night, she was searching for anything she could use against him. She went through his desk. She went through his car. She came upon the journal.

She shook him awake. "How dare you! How dare you say those lies about me?" He was now wide-awake. "Wait a minute. That was my private journal. I'm going to anger management class so I can get a grip on my anger."

"Lies, all lies! Just you wait," she screamed wildly. "I'm calling the police. I will tell them how you abused me—almost killed me with those scissors! And when I get finished with you, you won't even have a dental license! I'm going to the dental board. You're finished!"

He was livid. "You're a fucking bitch! You go right ahead. See who'll pay your fucking bills!"

He got out of bed, slammed the bedroom door, and slept in the spare bedroom the rest of the night. *Who the hell does she think she is? That bitch will get hers.* He thought all this to himself as he fell asleep, wishing his wife were dead

* * *

I walked into the office the next morning, and Dr. Jacobs immediately met me at the door. "Let me tell you her newest antic. She stole my journal out of my car and went ballistic when she read it." As he was describing, in great detail, the events of the previous night, all I could think of was, *enough is enough. No more yakking. Just do something already.*

"Look," I said. "That's enough already! You make each other miserable. Get out of the marriage!"

"I can't. She'll go to the police. She'll go to the dental board. I can't risk it. I have to just bide my time until she's miserable enough to leave. She keeps talking about buying a practice. Maybe she will. Then she'll go and my problems will be solved."

I don't know why I even bothered participating in such an absurd conversation. Nothing I said ever got through to him. This man, who was well over six feet tall, was desperately afraid of his five-foot wife, and the only way he could express it was through his anger. I actually felt sorry for him. For sure, he was a verbal abuser, and recently he had become a physical abuser. But still, I felt sorry for him. He was trapped in a misery of his own making, but he was convinced that everything was her fault. He had zero courage. He was truly pathetic. He believed she had the power to ruin him. Because of this fear, he was actually her slave. When he boiled over in anger, he played right into her hands. He gave her the ammunition she needed to emotionally blackmail him.

The rest of the day was exasperating. He was at my desk every chance he got. It was the same old stuff. "She did this, and she did that." I was sick of hearing it. Trying to shut him up did not work. He could continue talking, endlessly, even if I turned away and did other things. It was incredible. I needed to find the courage to leave. I just didn't have it in me. Maybe I did have it in me to write that book someday.

Dr. Tulip was intent on buying her own practice. The current big argument was over how he refused to co-sign for her. "Let her do it on her own," he reasoned. "If she can manage to find her own financing, then that's well and good for her. I'm not signing anything. Let her get her own practice, and then maybe she'll leave. Let her go."

The animosity between them was palpable. A constant heaviness hung over the office, as though it were a threatening cloud. Patients could sense it. We were losing patients every week. Every time we lost a patient, Dr. Tulip would blame Dr. Jacobs. "You do lousy work. They know you're no good. No wonder they're leaving."

"No, Babette, it's *you*. They hear you telling me that you don't want to see patients in *my* practice. Everyone knows you're crazy."

I began to feel that Dr. Tulip was not the only crazy one. It was obvious to Bill, to Kimmie, and to Marcie that something was wrong with me to continue staying there in the face of all this conflict. I was playing the role of counselor to Dr. Jacobs. I kept telling myself I needed to get out of there, but deep inside, I didn't want to. I wanted to see this situation to the end—whatever that was. Bill tried to understand me, but he just couldn't. "Lily, this situation is more than you can handle. You're consumed with it. Don't you at least want to think about leaving that place?"

I got quite annoyed when Bill started in on me about this. "NO, Bill! I will be out of there eventually, but now is not the time."

Frequently, after one of these disagreements with Bill, I would have the dream again. I was always back in my childhood home. My parents were always arguing. I wanted to fix it, but I was helpless. There was never anything I could do.

* * *

ALL OUT WAR

Chapter 16

Babette Tulip was upstairs, at her computer, writing an e-mail to her husband's therapist. "Again, I am writing to tell you that my husband's violent outbreaks are still continuing. I have written to you on several occasions, and you never answer my e-mails. This past weekend, he violently lost his temper in front of our kids. He called me a BITCH, A DRUNK, AND A WHORE. He also said he hated having sex with me. He said all of this in front of our children."

"I have told you many times how I believe he is on the wrong medication. I am a licensed dentist in the state of New Jersey, and I know about medications. He is on the wrong one! He was diagnosed years ago with Attention Deficit Disorder. You have him medicated for depression. If you would prescribe the right medication, perhaps he would go back to being the kind, loving man I married."

She continued with a vengeance. "I love my husband. I have been an excellent wife. I want him to be well again. However, his behavior is unacceptable. During his outbreaks, he says he doesn't love me, and he wants a divorce. I don't believe he really wants this. I know that, if he were properly medicated, our problems would be alleviated."

"Also, his work with his patients has been sloppy and unprofessional. If his bizarre behavior continues, I believe it may be my duty to report him to the State Dental Board. I also may have to report him to the police for his past physical abuse."

She was really wound up now. "Dr. Jacobs has completely abandoned our family. He leaves the house every night and goes to the cigar shop. He hangs out there all evening and doesn't return until ten o'clock at night." She ended the e-mail with, "I am telling you his medication is wrong and needs to be adjusted accordingly. Thank you, Dr. Babette Tulip." She clicked on *send*. She actually expected to get an answer.

* * *

Dr. Jacobs was at my desk early—before the first patient arrived. "She's totally nuts." I didn't have to ask about whom he was referring. He knew her password and had taken to routinely going into her e-mail account. Either she was really stupid or she didn't care. I entertained the thought that she wanted him to read her e-mails, possibly as a threat.

"She sent a letter to my therapist again," he continued. "I saw it in her e-mail account. She's off the wall if she thinks *my* therapist is going to answer her e-mails, or even discuss with her what goes on in my sessions. It's incredible. She takes no responsibility for our problems. She thinks all of our problems are because I have Attention Deficit Disorder. That doesn't even make sense. Here, Lily, read this latest e-mail."

"NO," I said emphatically. "I'm not going to read the e-mail. It's one thing for you to tell me about it, but I don't want to read it. It makes me feel really sleazy."

"Fine," he said. "I just wanted you to know how crazy she is."

"I know," I said. "You tell me that at least five times every day."

He continued complaining. He was going to the cigar shop almost nightly. It seemed there were a bunch of men who sat around smoking cigars and complaining about their wives. One of the guys gave him a book to read. It was called, *That Bitch* by Roy Sheppard and Mary T. Cleary. Dr. Jacobs insisted, "It describes my wife exactly. It seems like the book was written about her."

I really was feeling saturated with all of this. "You know, Dr. Jacobs, every day you give me a list of complaints about Dr. Tulip. Enough already! You're miserable. You tell me you hate her. You tell me she puts you through torture. When are you going to do something about it?"

"Lily, I know. I need to get stronger. I can't risk leaving now. What if she gets a restraining order against me? What if I can't practice here in my own house? What if she writes a letter to the dental board? What if she decides to press charges about the scissors I held to her throat months ago? I can't risk it. She's getting her own practice. Maybe then, I can get her to let go of this so-called marriage."

I had never seen cowardice quite like this. The man was totally terrorized by his wife. I didn't really understand it. I was getting quite sick of it.

"Well, Dr. Jacobs, you have two choices. Either live with it or shut up." It was amazing to me how I could talk to him in that manner. He had been telling me his really personal business for years now. He even told me things about his sex life. I never asked to be privy to any of this, and through it all, I was still supposed to call him "Dr. Jacobs." When did things become this crazy?

This man could not face any of his problems. He had a crazy, alcoholic wife who was making his life a living hell. She was picking at him constantly, criticizing and provoking him. She seemed to enjoy it when he lost his temper. Then she had something she could use to control him. He had a hot-blooded temper. He was not right to do the things he did. I knew he had once struck her. At least he told me it was only once, and he was sorry. I told him even once made him an abuser, and he had a problem. He said it had never happened before, and he was wrong, but of course, she had provoked him. The scissors incident was totally unacceptable, as well as being criminal. But she took pleasure in having something to hold over his head. She was free to leave, to end the marriage. She was a dentist. As bad as she was, she could still make a living on her own. But she clung to him, constantly threatening him. She had to be getting some kind of sadistic payoff from the situation.

He would not leave my desk. "I *will* get stronger, Lily." He continued at great length. "One day this will all be over. I'm not proud of the way I have acted. I was never violent. I can't believe I've turned into this person. I don't even know myself anymore." I was way beyond being annoyed with him, even though I did feel some degree of sympathy for his situation. He was so weak. He did have a terrible temper, but it seemed to come out of a feeling of helplessness. He was in over his head. He wanted out, but he sincerely believed he had no viable way to leave.

Interestingly, I never felt any sympathy at all for Dr. Babette Tulip. She was a true head case. She was the most vicious, narcissistic person I had ever encountered. She was also pathetic. She was actually trying to hold on to this sad marriage of theirs by threatening him. She was miserable and needy. In her mind, it was entirely his fault. If only she could change him, then everything would be better. She was determined, at all costs, to mold him into the husband she wanted him to be. If threatening him with going to the police would keep him in tow, then so be it.

I constantly wondered how long this could continue. Dr. Jacobs was beyond miserable. Dr. Tulip screamed at him and picked on him all day long. She was trying to provoke him. She was still talking about buying her own practice. She was convinced that a practice of her own would solve all of their problems. He was not going to co-sign a loan for her, but she kept trying to get approved on her own. Neither I nor Dr. Jacobs thought it would really happen. Dr. Jacobs told me it actually would be great if she could have her own practice. Then he could get rid of her. He wouldn't have to support her. The problem was she couldn't get credit on her own. He wasn't willing to financially back her. He couldn't trust her. He didn't want to be tied to her any more than he already was. Also, both Dr. Jacobs and I knew that Dr. Tulip did not know enough dentistry, or enough about business, to run her own practice.

The faxes were flying back and forth. Dr. Tulip started spending most of her day in pursuit of her own practice. All the while, she kept lecturing Dr. Jacobs how she wouldn't have to go through this if he would just give her a fair share of his practice. I was convinced that Dr. Tulip was delusional. Yes, the practice was in his name, but he never stopped her from seeing patients or doing any procedures she wanted. She chose not to do most procedures, and she needed to call him in for help on the rare occasion when she did any significant dentistry. When they had started this practice several years before, she agreed that the practice would be in his name. Her credit score was terrible. His was good, and it only made sense. All the profits were used to support their family. In addition, he actually gave her a paycheck that was quite sizeable. However, since the marriage had soured, this was one of her pet peeves—the practice was in his name only.

She was hell bent on owning her own practice. We soon learned that whatever Dr. Babette Tulip was determined to occur, would eventually come to pass.

Chapter 17

It actually happened. Dr. Tulip got approved for a loan on her own. Dr. Jacobs and I were both amazed that a bank would lend money to this unstable woman with a poor credit history. Nevertheless, she got the loan. She settled on an office space in a little strip mall about a mile from our office. I didn't think it was possible, but things actually became weirder than they already were.

Dr. Tulip no longer even made a pretense of seeing patients in our office. All day long, she was meeting with contractors. She wanted Dr. Jacobs' help in some ways, but most of the time she was quite secretive about what was going on at her new office. They both were in a sort of "la-la land." She kept saying this was going to be great for their marriage. She said she would finally be her own boss, and now they would get along beautifully. This woman had actually convinced herself that her marriage was really good, but circumstances had just created a few problems. When she wasn't around, he was talking my ear off about how, once Dr. Tulip was settled and earning her own money, he was going to get out of the marriage. He still told me constantly that she was an alcoholic, and to prove it, he took pictures of liquor bottles he found stashed under furniture. Somehow, he thought this was going to help him in the inevitable divorce that would certainly be in their future.

Everything went from bad to worse. They started fighting over dental equipment. She would ask for his help and then go and do the opposite from what he advised her to do. Most of the time, her decisions were hasty and ill thought out. He told her to order equipment from the dental supply house he always used. She told him to "bug off," and then she spent hours ordering old equipment from eBay. Equipment started arriving, and she insisted it be stored in our already over-crowded office, because her office was not yet finished. He complained to me that she was "crazy." She began hanging around my desk whenever she was in the office and complaining how he was bossy and controlling. She never used to hang around my desk. But now, she seemed to want to get her side of the story in. Perhaps she suspected he was confiding in me.

According to him, she was now drunk almost every night. His lawyer instructed him to call the police when he saw his wife in a drunken stupor. That sounded bizarre to me, but Dr. Jacobs said his lawyer wanted to get it on record that Dr. Tulip was an alcoholic. Unfortunately, this did not exactly go as Dr. Jacobs and his lawyer had planned.

* * *

They were upstairs. She had been drinking all evening. She was totally wasted. As usual, she began chastising him for anything and everything she could think of. He called the police. When they arrived, she was clearly drunk. She was so drunk that she actually threw up right in front of the officers. She ran into the bathroom. "See," Dr. Jacobs pleaded, "she's like this every night. My kids are home. Is there anything you can do?" To Dr. Jacobs' great disappointment, he found out it was not illegal for anyone to be drunk in his or her own home.

* * *

She started telling him she wanted a lot of little supplies from our office. She said she was entitled to them. Huge fights ensued. The atmosphere in the office got more and more hostile. I could only imagine what the atmosphere was like upstairs. Every morning, he would come downstairs with a whole list of complaints. It seemed as though he couldn't wait to unload them on me. I continued to question and to doubt myself. *Why am I still here?* I felt more than stuck. I felt paralyzed. Even though I no longer believed I could fix anything about this situation, a big part of me wanted to stay to see how this terrible, ugly mess would eventually turn out. And of course, I always made a mental note how this would make a great book.

I told him over and over again that, if he were that miserable, he should get out of the marriage. It was like talking to a stone. He was waiting. He wanted her to make her own money. He kept thinking she would eventually want out of the marriage, and all he had to do was wait. All the while, she kept threatening him over the scissors incident that had occurred months before. She seemed to love having something to hold over his head. It was so obvious to me she did not want out of the marriage. She wanted to control him. She was obsessed with him. No matter how miserable things were, she was never going to let him go. He told me that, after every nasty fight, she would later ask, "Do you still love me?"

My reaction was, "You've got to be kidding. What do you tell her?"

"Simple," he said. "I just tell her, 'Yeah, I love you.'"

She insisted on knowing his every move. She wanted to know where he was at all times. According to him, he wasn't even allowed to watch a TV show without her. I thought he must surely be exaggerating, but then I saw an example of her paranoid jealousy.

It was their custom to attend a dental study club once a month. Usually, it was a lecture about some type of dental procedure. They got a free lunch out of it, as well as continuing education credits. At one of the sessions, Dr. Jacobs told a female sales rep he needed an adjustment on a small piece of equipment called a hand piece. Apparently, this sales rep was extremely attractive, and Dr. Tulip thought the rep was coming on to Dr. Jacobs. A few days later, the rep called the office and said she was going to be in the neighborhood and would like to stop by and look at the hand piece. Of course I agreed. I had no idea this was a powder keg waiting to blow.

Dr. Jacobs was in his operatory with a patient. Dr. Tulip was upstairs doing whatever Dr. Tulip did when she was upstairs. Jill, the rep, came into the office. Dr. Tulip came running down the back stairs and confronted Jill. In her sugary-sweet, fake voice she cooed. "Why, Jill, so lovely to see you! Exactly what brings you here?" Jill explained she was there to inspect the hand piece. Dr. Jacobs excused himself from his patient and came out to the waiting area. He showed Jill the hand piece. Actually, it had been acting up all week, but this time it was working just fine. Dr. Tulip looked pleased with herself. Jill left. Dr. Jacobs went back to his patient. Dr. Tulip came over to my desk and said, "That bitch was coming on to my husband at the study club. She wasn't in the neighborhood. She was just hitting on my husband." The whole thing was so ridiculous. Reps stopped by all the time. This one was *not* interested in Dr. Jacobs. She was simply doing her job. Dr. Tulip had a wild look in her eye. "He better not ever cheat on me!" It was really bizarre. The marriage was miserable. She treated him like dirt, but she was holding on for dear life. He was her possession, and she was not letting go.

Dr. Jacobs could hardly fit the description of a prized possession. He was no great catch. He was completely neurotic and had a huge temper. He was controlling in his own right. However, he had surrendered his soul to this crazy woman. He hated her but allowed himself to be in a position where she could hold onto him with threats. He reiterated to me once again that, if he left her, she would go to the police and say all kinds of things. Theirs was the most toxic relationship I had ever witnessed.

Every evening I would come home exhausted. It wasn't so much that the work was making me tired. It was the exhausting situation. Bill was no longer amused when I told him what was going on at the office. "Okay, Lily, you need to quit." He started being more forceful in his statements. "This so-called job is making you sick. There's no reason for you to be in the middle of their pathetic situation. If you won't quit, then at least tell Dr. Jacobs to shut up and keep you out of it."

But I could not do as Bill asked. It was hard for me to explain to Bill, or even to myself, for that matter, why I continued to stay. I knew deep in my conscious that Dr. Jacobs reminded me a little of my father—a good man, but unable to control his temper when caught up in what he perceived as a hopeless situation. I wanted to help Dr. Jacobs in some way. I felt that by letting him vent to me, I was helping the situation. I didn't realize that I was not helping—just enabling.

As Dr. Tulip was getting her office ready to launch, things were getting tenser and tenser. More and more small pieces of equipment started disappearing from our office. He accused her of taking them to her new location. Huge fights constantly erupted. She was always accusing him of being jealous of her having a new office, and he should be supporting her, not condemning her. He continued to tell me that she was making really stupid decisions and he could not wait to be rid of her. He continued telling me on more than one occasion how he wished she were dead.

Dr. Tulip told me to run an ad for an office manager for her new office. I screened the applicants for her, all the while knowing these potential employees had no idea what they would be getting themselves into. We had several interviews. She wanted me to sit in. She said she wanted my opinion. Yeah right! That would be the day, when Dr. Babette Tulip asked my opinion for anything.

Ramona Green walked into the office for an interview. She was a formidable woman. Her presence filled the room. Immediately, she struck me as the same personality type as Dr. Tulip. I was right. Dr. Tulip had met her match. The interview was a bragging contest. Dr. Tulip talked about what a great dentist she was and how she was going to help her husband by referring root canal patients back to our office. Dr. Jacobs loved doing root canals. He tried to do all but the most difficult cases. He also loved the money that root canals brought into the office. He would only refer the really complicated ones to Dr. Steiner, the endodontist. Dr. Tulip knew not to even attempt root canals. She actually believed herself when she told Ramona about cooperating with Dr. Jacobs and referring root canals back to our office. Ramona kept nodding in agreement. I could tell she was thinking what a great wife and dentist her new prospective employer was.

Ramona had worked for a well-known dentist, Dr. Cameron, for ten years. Dr. Cameron had retired, and Ramona didn't care for the new, younger dentist who bought the practice. She bragged to Dr. Tulip how she had done everything for Dr. Cameron. "That man never had to worry about anything," she said, singing her own praises. "He never had to open a bill. All he needed to do was practice dentistry. I took care of everything. I ran the office completely. I made life easy for Dr. Cameron. He didn't have to worry about a thing."

As Ramona was boasting, I was thinking how this situation was made to order for Dr. Tulip. She knew nothing about running a business. She couldn't even put an appointment in the computer. Of course, it was fraught with perils. How could you trust someone to do the books when there was no system of checks and balances in place?

Dr. Tulip was totally enamored of Ramona. If I hadn't seen what happened next, I would not have believed it. Dr. Tulip stood up and waved her arms wildly in the air. "I have Ramona! I have Ramona!" She waved her arms rapidly and screamed like a wild woman. This was quite a match. Dr. Tulip had found a redeemer. She found someone who would make all business decisions for her. On the other hand, Ramona found someone who would let her have autonomy in the office and give her even more to boast about.

Ramona was hired, and Dr. Tulip devoted herself to getting her new office ready. The equipment was arriving from eBay almost daily. Some of it was really old. Dr. Jacobs was amazed by Dr. Tulip's method of acquiring things so haphazardly. The equipment took up all kinds of room in our office, because Dr. Tulip's office wasn't ready yet. She said she couldn't store it in her new office, because the floor had not yet been laid.

All the while, the fights continued. The doctors were extremely nasty to one another. Dr. Jacobs looked awful. He was oversleeping. I would call upstairs when his first patient arrived in the morning and find I had awakened him with my phone call. His excuse was, "The bitch let me oversleep. She deliberately turned off my alarm." He took absolutely no responsibility for his own carelessness.

Dr. Tulip was extremely hyper. In between her appointments for Botox injections, she ran back and forth to her new, soon-to-be opened office to meet with different contractors. She was so arrogant! When she was in our office, I actually heard her tell one of Dr. Jacobs' patients that she was the better dentist. And, as if that weren't enough, she added how, after the move, they should come to her new office instead of staying with Dr. Jacobs. She actually thought that sort of tactic would win her future patients. The outcome was just the reverse. We kept losing patients, and there was no guarantee they would surface again when Dr. Tulip's new office opened.

Dr. Jacobs believed all he had to do was wait. He convinced himself that once she had her own office, he would be free of her. He thought she would be happy, and all of her threats would be long gone. He could not have been more wrong.

Chapter 18

D r. Tulip's new office was complete. Dr. Jacobs actually helped her move in. I stopped by to see it. It was glitzy. She may have bought used equipment from eBay, but the décor in her office was anything but second hand. It had blue microfiber sofas and beautiful wood tables. The reception area showed off granite counters, and even I had to admit the office was beautiful. Dr. Tulip was one of the un-classiest people I had ever known, but she actually did a good job of making this office look elegant and upscale. I knew for a fact that she was an inadequate dentist. To say the least, she had very limited ability with performing restorative procedures. There was quite a contrast between the look of the office, and the ability of the dentist who planned to practice there.

Dr. Tulip having her own office did not make life more harmonious between herself and her husband. I could hear them fighting upstairs when I came to work in the morning. She didn't seem to leave to go to her new office until nine or ten o'clock. Dr. Jacobs and I wondered what exactly she was doing there. She would come home midday for about two hours. He said she wouldn't tell him anything about patient volume, or even if she had any patients. Their fights were getting worse and worse. In addition, small pieces of equipment continued to disappear from our office. When he would confront her, she would usually deny taking anything. Sometimes, however, she would admit taking something, and then say, "It's half mine, anyway. You forced me out of this office, so I have a right to take anything I want." She had a really convenient memory. For years now, she had been saying she wanted to have her own office, and she wanted to be her own boss. Now she said she had been forced out.

They continually fought over who owned which patients. Since she had cleaned the teeth of every patient in the practice, she claimed they were exclusively her patients. The concept was utterly ridiculous. He did almost all of the real dental work. She hardly ever did any fillings or crowns. She never did a bridge or a denture.

Every morning, when I came to work, I wondered what the fight of the day would be. Dr. Jacobs would come downstairs from the house (usually late) and give me another reason why he hated his wife—how she was stealing supplies from his office to take to her new office and how they were fighting over patients, etc. He would always add how he wished she were dead. Every day, I would ask him why he didn't just end the misery and ask for a divorce. Every day he would tell me he was trapped, and if he left, she would make up lies about him and report him to the police for lots of abuse—most of it made up. I wondered how long this could go on. The atmosphere in the office was positively poisonous. I couldn't shake the feeling that, at any minute, things could really blow. I had no idea just how huge the impending disaster would be.

To say the situation was strange was an enormous understatement. In the middle of all the tension, Dr. Jacobs told me that he and Dr. Tulip and the kids were going away to Florida for spring break. I couldn't believe what I was hearing. They were constantly fighting with each other. He was telling me how he hated her and was hoping she would come to her senses and leave the marriage. He was afraid to take the initiative. He was terrified she would make good on her blackmail threats. Why were these people taking a vacation together? The logic was beyond me. He felt he needed to do everything she said. She was totally out of touch and was trying desperately to hold on to him. She was sick enough to think she could accomplish her goal by threats. According to him, she was in a drunken stupor every night. Her behavior was becoming increasingly more bizarre. Actually, I did believe she would never let him go. She was so completely obsessed with him that she wanted to control him body and soul. If she couldn't control him with sex, then she was going to accomplish control by blackmail. She knew she was losing him. She was a desperate woman.

Dr. Jacobs looked tired and beat. "Tell me exactly why you are going to Florida?" I asked again. I had long ago stopped pretending I was not interested. Actually, I felt like I was observing a never-ending soap opera. I wanted to find out what would happen next. Also, there was always that book I might write someday. "Lily, you know why I have to go to Florida," he reiterated once again. "She's a loose cannon. She's threatening me every day now. She knows I'm done with her, but she just won't let go. In her sick way, she still wants me. I need time to make her come to the realization that a divorce is best for both of us. If I just leave the marriage, who knows what will happen? She will probably go off the deep end. I'm taking the family to Florida, just as she wants."

I heard his words, but I still had a hard time understanding exactly what he was thinking. What could she possibly do? The scissors incident had happened over a year ago. Why was he so afraid of her? I knew she was vicious. I knew she was vindictive. But this man was truly frozen in fear. Of course, he was not exactly sane, either. He was such a coward! He would whine and complain all day to anyone who would listen. He could be bossy and controlling in his own right. Yet he was clearly miserable and wanted nothing more to do with her. It was such a bizarre situation. He supposedly was the abuser. Yet, he was the one who wanted out. He said he wished he would never have to see her again. She, on the other hand, while claiming that he had abused her, clung to this dead marriage.

The practice continued to suffer severely. More and more patients asked to have their records forwarded to other dentists. Dr. Jacobs could never see his responsibility in any of this. He would often just scream about the patients being ungrateful for all the wonderful care he had given them. He could not see what a sick place the office had become. He came downstairs later and later each morning. Even after I would call upstairs and tell him there was a patient waiting, he would take another twenty minutes before he finally presented himself.

The family left for Florida. I could only imagine what kind of trip it would turn out to be.

* * *

They were just returning to their hotel room after an afternoon on the beach. He had actually had a nice day. "You know, Babette today wasn't bad at all. The kids had a great time."

She also tried to be soft spoken. "Yes, they did, didn't they, Robert?" She seemed to be making an effort. He thought that maybe this vacation was making her start to mellow. She had been in a good mood since they left home. She wasn't at all the bitchy, nagging, vengeful woman he had come to know of late. Maybe she had seen the error of her ways? Could he even hope for that?

Later that evening, when the boys had fallen asleep, she climbed on top of him as they lay under the covers. She was like an animal in heat. He loved it.

She stayed awake afterwards. She smiled to herself, as she thought how easy it was to manipulate his trust. He was like a child—one that could be yanked around just like a puppet. That was her plan. Let him think that everything was going to be okay. It was all coming together, now. He had treated her poorly all those years. He wouldn't give her what was rightfully hers —a share of the practice they had built together. Furthermore, she was *never* going to forget how he held that scissors to her throat. He was even more stupid than she had thought, if he assumed even for a minute that she would forget that whole business with the scissors. Let him think everything was fine for now. He would get a surprise when they all returned home from vacation.

* * *

The office was eerily quiet. The family was on vacation, and I was "minding the store." I had plenty of work to do—answering the phone, catching up on my filing. I wondered how things would be when they returned. I hoped they didn't have terrible fights in front of the children. Maybe the vacation did them both some good, and hateful behavior on both their sides would subside. In my heart, I knew that wouldn't happen. I knew that the situation was not "if" things would blow wide open, but "when" and "how."

The whole time they were gone, we continued to lose patients. Some of the patients who called for their records to be transferred were not afraid to tell me that the atmosphere in our office was just plain unacceptable. I didn't blame them one bit. Who wanted a dentist who talked about his personal problems while his patient is in his chair? Who wanted to visit their dentist and be caught in the middle of rude looks and snide remarks being flung back and forth between the two practitioners?

The practice did, however, have its share of loyal patients. Knowing how I was the only one in the office for the week, some patients who called wanted to discuss the situation. Even though I was uncomfortable with this, I knew that Dr. Jacobs had already told them in great detail about his personal life. Some patients just wanted to tell me they would stick with Dr. Jacobs no matter what. Other patients wanted to make certain their records would be transferred over to Dr. Tulip's new office. It was a turbulent time. I knew it was not going to get any better.

NO TURNING BACK
(SO WATCH YOUR BACK)

Chapter 19

S pring break was over and the family came back from Florida. Dr. Jacobs actually told me that all had been quiet while they were away. No real fighting had occurred. This was a very temporary state of affairs. They had not been back one day, when the first of many patients came in holding a letter that, apparently, Dr. Tulip had sent to them. It was a hastily done thing that Dr. Tulip must have thrown together while she was drinking. There were multiple misspellings. It explained how she was no longer with the practice at our address, and it encouraged patients to call her office manager, Ramona, and have their records transferred over to her new office. It sounded as though the whole practice had been moved over to her new office.

Dr. Jacobs was livid. "While we were on vacation, she was having her office send these damn flyers out. She has no right to solicit my patients! All she ever did was clean their damn teeth. She never did any real work around here." He was angrier than I had ever seen him. "Damn fucking bitch!"

They didn't even try to hide their fighting from me. He accused her of sabotaging his practice by trying to steal his patients. "You should be happy to help me," she retorted. "You're jealous of any success I might have!" She wouldn't address the issue of how she was helping him if she stripped his office of patients.

The tension in the office was like a gray cloud of gloom permeating everything and everyone. Even though Dr. Tulip was working in her own office most of the day, her presence was felt everywhere in our office. Dr. Jacobs talked about her all day long. "She's a drunk. She's a whore. Why doesn't she just get the hell out of my life? The boys and I would be better off without her." Of course, these were all rhetorical questions. My usual response was, "Why don't you just tell her you want a divorce? Why don't you just leave? Why don't you stop complaining and do something?"

Of course, he always had the same answer. If he left, she would make his life so miserable, that it wouldn't be worth living. She would go to the police. She would make up charges. She would go after his license. The list would go on, and on, and on. He was convinced she would eventually see the light and leave on her own. He was further convinced she would let him have custody of the boys. I knew he was delusional about that. One thing was for certain about Dr. Jacobs. When he believed he was right, he assumed the universe would eventually see it his way and things would be just like he said. I knew Dr. Tulip was not going to give up on him. She would continue to attempt to turn him into what she wanted him to be. Along the way, she could possible destroy all of them.

I was stuck inside a terrible drama. I wasn't exactly sure why, but I felt almost paralyzed with dread. I could not bring myself to leave, yet I had a sinking feeling that something awful could happen at any time. Furthermore, I had somehow become sympathetic to this neurotic, sad figure of a man. He was a dope. He needed to stand up for himself. It was pathetic. In the midst of all of this, he would tell me that she would grope him in the middle of the night. "Dr. Jacobs! That is *too much information!*" I could not believe that even he would tell me such things, nor did I want to know the particulars of their sex life. These people were out to destroy each other, but in some weird way, they apparently still connected in the bedroom. It continued to be obvious to me that she would never let him go. I knew he hated her. Even though she was a conniving, two-faced liar (I really believed this to be true), I felt it was wrong for anyone to talk about his or her spouse the way he did. I knew she sensed that she had lost him. I supposed the only way she could still maintain a connection with him was through sex. She would constantly insist that he tell her he loved her. It was incredible. He would tell her what she wanted to hear.

I often felt that Dr. Jacobs was either really stupid or perhaps he had blinders on. His mind was like a steel trap. He could remember every detail about every patient, but he had no common sense. He couldn't see how he needed to take control before this sick, bitchy, vengeful, alcoholic woman drove him to the point of no return. He found it difficult to see his own responsibility in this terrible situation. He was a controlling, bossy, but naïve, individual. She was more than ten years older than he was. She knew his vulnerabilities and she used them well.

I knew this situation could not continue, but I had no idea of the manner in which it would all disintegrate.

* * *

Chapter 20

It was late at night. As usual Babette had been drinking—an entire bottle of wine, a fifth of gin. She fell asleep on their bed. As was her custom, she took the younger boy to bed with her. Robert picked up his sleeping son and carried him down the hall to the boy's own bed. He tucked Teddy in bed. He went back into their bedroom. He gazed at his passed-out wife. He despised her when she was drunk. Rage and helplessness welled up inside him. She was harming the children. She used Teddy as her own personal shield. Robert never suspected anything sexual was going on between his wife and his younger son, but he knew that psychological damage was occurring when she babied the boy and made him feel as though he had to protect his mother in some way. How could she do such damage to her own son? This practice of sleeping with the boy, or rather passing out while taking Teddy to bed with her, must stop. A lot of things had to stop. He needed to find a way to leave. He had to find the strength. He was tired—so very tired. He crawled into his side of the bed. He could smell the liquor on her breath. A wave of revulsion rose up inside him.

It was the middle of the night. She awoke and reached over to him. He turned his back to her. She forcefully attempted to roll him back towards her. He resisted. She grabbed for his crotch. He heard her moan. "Come on, you know you want me. You know you love me." He could still smell the liquor on her breath. He was repulsed. "Babette, get the fuck off me!" He didn't even realize the depth of his anger he let loose. "You're a fucking, blackmailing whore! I hate your fucking guts, and I want a divorce!" With that, he pushed her aside and got up from the bed.

She got out of the bed and ran after him. "You want a divorce, do you? I'll give you your divorce, but you're going down the tubes, you son of a bitch." She then picked up a high-heeled slipper from the floor and started pounding on his back. He threw her off. "You're a crazy drunk. I wish you were dead." He slammed the door to the bedroom and headed down the hall to sleep in the spare room.

The next morning, things were strangely quiet. There were no morning accusations, no incriminating looks, nothing. Dr. Jacobs wondered why. Usually, after one of their ferocious fights, she was right there in the morning, ready to continue the battle. That didn't happen this morning. He wondered about that. He also hoped that, somehow, Justin and Teddy had not heard what happened between their parents.

* * *

She left the house early for work at her new office. He saw to his morning patients. "Well, Lily, we had another one of our famous fights last night." I wasn't in the mood to hear it. "Tell me another time," I said. "I've got insurance claims to process." I was really getting tired of this.

The afternoon was going to be slow. After we broke for lunch, there would not be another patient until the end of the day. I had things I wanted to do. He didn't care if I took the afternoon off. I was paid by the hour, so it was a winning situation for him. He didn't have to pay me for the hours I wasn't there.

He came back from lunch and saw a note on the reception desk. It was a card from the county sheriff. It said, "Robert, please call me at the following number."

"What the fuck?" Dr. Jacobs yelled. "What the fuck has that bitch done now?" Of course, any sensible person would have called the number on the card. However, by no stretch of the imagination could anyone ever call Dr. Robert Z. Jacobs sensible. He had an inkling of what was actually happening. He went upstairs to the house and took a pair of pants and a shirt. Then he thought he knew what he should do. In about five minutes he was barging through the door of Dr. Tulip's new office.

"Where is she? Get her out here!"

Ramona Green lifted her formidable body out of her chair. "Dr. Jacobs, Dr. Tulip is with a patient right now. Can I help you?" Dr. Tulip had told her office manager how Dr. Jacobs was an abuser with a nasty temper. Ramona believed every word of it. "Dr. Jacobs," she persisted, "calm down. Dr. Tulip is with a patient."

"Ramona, get her out here now!" Just then, Dr. Tulip appeared. "Ramona, call the sheriff's department. Tell them Dr. Jacobs is here and he is violent."

To Dr. Jacobs, all of this was like waving a red flag in front of a bull. He would not quit. "What the fuck do you think you're doing? What is this card from the sheriff's office?"

"You'll see, Robert, you'll see. I warned you," Dr. Tulip retorted. After several minutes of cursing, Dr. Jacobs turned on his heels, walked out the door of his wife's office, and bumped right into the sheriff, who promptly served him with a restraining order.

The note on the reception desk instructed him to call the sheriff. Of course, as always, Dr. Jacobs' temper got the better of him, and now he was really in trouble. Ramona Green was a witness to his temper, as was Dr. Tulip's patient.

* * *

Dr. Jacobs called me that night. He was shouting. He told me what had transpired at Dr. Tulip's office.

"You did what?" I could not believe how stupid this man could be. "Why didn't you just call the number on the card like you were supposed to? Now they are going to say that you disrupted her office with your temper."

"Look, Lily," he said, "I have enough aggravation as it is. Don't you now start giving me grief." That was so very typical of Dr. Jacobs. He never took responsibility for anything he did. Somehow, he was going to justify barging in at Dr. Tulip's office.

"What exactly does all this mean?" I asked.

"It means she made it sound like the old scissors incident had just happened. It means the fucking bitch is making up all kinds of lies. The order says I can only be in my office weekdays from nine to five. I have to stay away from her, and since the office is in the basement of the house,

I'm locked out of the house when it is not regular office hours."

This presented a huge problem. Regular office hours were from eight to five. All of the eight o'clock patients would have to be cancelled, and some of the late afternoon patients too. He wouldn't be able to start any procedures in the afternoon, unless they were finished before five o'clock. He could be arrested for being in violation of the restraining order if he stayed in the office even one minute after five. He was livid. He couldn't get through the day without saying "fucking bitch" under his breath and usually out loud about every ten minutes. He refused to see his responsibility in any of this. In his mind, this "bitch," this "whore," this worthless "piece of shit" had driven him to do whatever it was he did. I reminded him again how it had been a big mistake for him to go over to her office, but he only got angrier. "I needed to find out what the hell she had done."

"You needed to call the sheriff's office," I countered. "That's what the card told you to do. The explosion in her office will only come back to haunt you." He wasn't hearing anything I said. It was true. She was an unbalanced, narcissistic whack job. But he was feeding right into her hands. She always was out to prove he had an uncontrollable temper. By his actions, he proved her right.

I read the restraining order. She had thrown everything in there. Besides making the old scissors incident sound like it had just recently happened, she accused him of all kinds of physical abuse. I could tell that most of it was made up. I knew him. He was a big blowhard. He was all scream and cussing, but with no bite. She told the police how afraid of him she was. I had been with them for several years now. I knew she was definitely not afraid of him. I also knew that, now that the "floodgates of hell" had been opened, there would be no turning back.

* * *

I had the dream again. *I was back in the house where I had grown up. My parents were going at it again. My mother was accusing my father of all kinds of wrongdoing. He didn't make enough money. He was a failure. She was criticizing everything about him. He looked like he was going to strike her, but he never did. Why didn't she stop? Why did she keep doing that? Why was she never happy with what he did or anyone else for that matter? My father came back at her with his usual verbal assaults. "Stop, Daddy. Please stop! Don't you know that if you continue, Mommy will leave again? She always leaves after one of these fights. Yes, she comes back, but it's scary in the house when I come home from school and she's not there. Don't do it, Daddy! I know she says mean things to you, but when you call her bad names, it gets worse."*

* * *

I suddenly awoke in a cold sweat. Bill was sleeping peacefully next to me. I lay awake and thought about the dream. I really did know deep inside why I tolerated life in that crazy dental office. It was strange, but Dr. Jacobs was weak and powerless, the way my father had been. My father was a good man, but he could not stand up to my mother's manipulative ways. He handled his frustration by verbally lashing out. My father never got physical with my mother, but the verbal abuse was always there. My mother was depressed. She blamed my father for all that was wrong in her life. She taunted and criticized him constantly, and the vicious cycle perpetuated itself. I had thought of all this before, but this time it was clearer than ever. I didn't know where I was going with all of this awareness, but I felt that, with each dream, I was gaining more understanding of the extreme madness in that office. More importantly, I was gaining insight into my own reasons for staying.

I didn't know how all of this would eventually end. I kept hoping the situation would work itself out. I really thought Dr. Tulip placed the restraining order just for spite. She wanted to teach him a lesson. She wanted him to know how powerful she could be. I believed she was waiting for him to beg her forgiveness and then she planned to triumphantly return to him. I knew, however, that Dr. Jacobs was never going to beg her forgiveness. Furthermore, he was never going to forgive her for what she did to him. The restraining order was ruining his livelihood. She had crossed the line (just as he had when he threatened her with the scissors). I believed this time that the marriage was truly over, but how things would play out, was anyone's guess.

HOW LOW CAN YOU GO?

Chapter 21

D r. Jacobs was extremely disturbed and agitated. He ranted and raved to anyone who was unfortunate enough to be within earshot, and that included his patients. Due to the restraining order, he could only be in the basement part of the house where the office was located, and only during specified hours. He was denied access to the main part of the house. He actually asked me if he could sleep in my guest room. Of course I said no. I couldn't believe he had the nerve to ask me that. So now, he was sleeping on an acquaintance's couch. It was a guy he had met at the cigar shop where he often hung out. That guy had offered him his couch, and Dr. Jacobs didn't have too many options. He had already lost a lot of patients, when Dr. Tulip opened her own office and solicited so many patients from our office. Now he was losing even more. It never occurred to him that some patients were leaving because they were just plain sick of hearing him talk about his messy personal problems.

I knew I was sick of hearing him. I did, however, still have some sympathy for him. I felt bad about his having to cancel all of his eight o'clock patients and not being able to schedule any lengthy procedures after three o'clock in the afternoon. He complained constantly from the moment I saw him in the morning, until he left at five o'clock in the afternoon. I had to close up the office myself, so he could be out of there according to the terms of the restraining order. The restraining order was to be in effect for a year. If he behaved himself, then it would be lifted after that time. He was allowed visitation with Justin and Teddy two times a week, and every other weekend. He was to be in his car on Monday and Wednesday evenings at six o'clock. He was instructed to pull up in front of the house and honk. Babette was supposed to send the kids out.

Right away, there was trouble with this arrangement. She said that Teddy did not want to see his father and she was *not* going to send him out. Dr. Jacobs had a lawyer—a one Nathaniel Batt. Mr. Batt advised Dr. Jacobs to sit tight. Things were prejudiced against him while the restraining order was in place.

Just how prejudiced the system was against Dr. Jacobs due to the restraining order was soon evident. The order had been in place for about two weeks. It was on a Friday night, a little over a week and a half since the order was issued. I got a call on my cell phone. "Lily, it's Dr. Jacobs." (Nothing, and I mean nothing, ever gave Dr. Jacobs the slightest inkling that he should tell me to call him Robert.) "I'm being arrested. I was at the cigar shop, and two cops came in, read me my rights, and I'm in the parking lot now. They're about to take me in. Call my lawyer—please."

Before I could even say, "What happened?" he hung up.

I called Nathaniel Batt, but, of course, all I got was his answering machine. I left him a message. Then I waited out most of the weekend to see what would happen next. There was no turning back. I was going to stick around long enough to see how all of this turned out.

Bill knew that any attempts to get me to quit my job at this point would be utterly futile.

"Lily, at least try to stop thinking about this situation every waking moment of every day." Recently, I had been on edge most of the time. I was having difficulty leaving all the problems at the office. I couldn't stop thinking about them, so the stress followed me when I got home. Bill tried to tell me once again. "Lily, their problems are not your problems. I am well aware I can't make you leave, but thinking about those lunatics all the time is making you sick." I knew what Bill was saying. I even agreed with him. That still didn't change anything.

I got a call from Dr. Jacobs on Sunday night. He had spent the night in lockup. His wife had brought more charges against him for breaking the restraining order. He said she had made ridiculous accusations against him. He would tell me about them later. Nathaniel Batt couldn't get him out of jail until the next day. Dr. Jacobs needed to post five thousand dollars for his own bail. He went before a judge who (according to Dr. Jacobs) treated him as though he were the scum of the earth. He was ordered not to go near the house at all—not even the office part. Nathaniel Batt pointed out that Dr. Jacobs' livelihood was in the basement of that house. The judge was unimpressed.

Dr. Jacobs would have to stay away until his trial. The charges for breaking the restraining order were considered to be criminal charges.

Of course, I wanted to know exactly what the charges were. Dr. Jacobs said he would tell me about them, later, but in the meantime, he needed me to go to work in the morning and cancel all of his appointments until Nathaniel Batt could do something for him. He thought it wouldn't be more than a day or two before he could get back into the office.

Wow, was he ever wrong! Each day, I came into the office and cancelled the patients for the following day. It was a grueling task. I couldn't even tell the patients when they would be able to get back in to see the dentist. Each afternoon, a despondent Dr. Jacobs would call me and tell me to continue to cancel the patients for yet another day. This went on for two weeks. By that time, we had lost three new patients and about ten more patients who were just fed-up with the whole situation. To make matters even worse than they already were, while Dr. Jacobs had been barred from his office, faxes had come in requesting patient records. They were patients who had been at our office, but were now seeing Dr. Tulip at her new office. Of course, I couldn't release any records without Dr. Jacobs signing off on them. He couldn't sign off on them. He wasn't allowed in his office! Dr. Tulip filed charges with the dental board, accusing Dr. Jacobs of not releasing records. Was she kidding? This was really absurd. Dr. Jacobs did call the dental board and he told them what had happened. "How can I release records when I can't even get into my office?" I was beginning to understand why he had been so afraid of what she could do. There didn't seem to be any end to her vindictiveness. As it turned out, the dental board did dismiss those particular charges, but there was still plenty to be concerned about.

Finally, a judge heard his case to get back into the office so he could continue his livelihood. He was allowed back in, but this time, the judge stipulated only on workdays from eight in the morning until six o'clock in the evening. He couldn't stay late in the evening to do paper work or get into his office at all on the weekend. He had lost two weeks of work, several patients, and he was raving mad.

"What the fuck does that bitch think she's doing? I want to see her dead! It's bad enough that cheating bitch took my patients. It's bad enough she had me barred from my office for two weeks. I'm still facing criminal charges for her trumped-up accusations. Now, she's using Teddy against me." Even though Dr. Jacobs had been granted permission to see his kids twice a week and every other weekend, Babette had said that Teddy, the younger one, was afraid of his father, and she was not going to let the younger boy be traumatized by visitations. Apparently, because of the restraining order, she could get away with that.

It was obvious that Dr. Jacobs was truly blinded by rage. Instead of thinking how he could get himself out of this mess, he was constantly going on and on about how the bitch did this and the bitch did that. He refused, or just could not admit to his own part in this chaos. He had lost a huge percentage of patients. There was a restraining order against him. In addition, there were criminal charges pending for breaking that restraining order. Every patient who came in had to suffer through his ranting about his insane, soon-to-be ex-wife. After his arrest, he finally filed for divorce. (It was about time. I thought he should have done that long ago, before the situation ever got this bad.) Again, I asked him what the criminal charges were that she had filed against him. "Would you believe," he said, "the criminal charges were for going into the house and getting a shirt and pants, after I discovered the card from the sheriff's office."

"But you hadn't even been served at that point," I noted.

"You got that right," he said. "They'll have to drop those charges, if I can get anyone to even listen to me."

The whole situation was incredibly difficult. Dr. Tulip and the children were still living in the house. Dr. Jacobs was only allowed to come into the office part of the house. They were separated, but still in close proximity to each other. That alone came with its own set of problems. It actually seemed as though she wanted to see him as road kill. One patient, Carl, was due to have sixteen thousand dollars worth of restorative work done. Dr. Jacobs could hardly wait. He desperately needed the money. Carl showed up the morning of his appointment as scheduled. Dr. Tulip had not left for her office yet, so she was still in the house. Apparently, she saw Carl start to open the door to the office. At one time, she had cleaned his teeth. She yelled to him from the front door of the house. He went up to talk to her. I don't know what she said to him, but about ten minutes later, Carl got in his car and drove off. Dr. Jacobs was screaming about it the rest of the day. Because of her, he had lost another patient—one that was about to have some very expensive work done. I have to admit, this time, I agreed with him. She had gone way too far.

At dinner, after one especially trying day at that insane place where I worked, Bill again asked me why I was so determined to ride it out. "I have to stay," I retorted. "We've been through this before, Bill."

"I know, Lily," he said. "I understand you wish you could fix things there, but you can't. Their situation is a lot different than your parents' situation was. You definitely could not fix your parents. That whole scenario was not your fault, and you sure as hell cannot fix this crazy situation at work."

"I know that, Bill," I said, "but there are other reasons I can't leave."

"What other reasons, Lily?"

"Well, for one thing, I need to stick around to see how this crazy thing finally ends," I answered as best I could. "Also, I really do think this would make some really wild story, if I ever do get around to writing that book I keep talking about. I could not make this stuff up."

"Well," Bill said, "I hope you're taking good notes."

* * *

Chapter 22

Babette looked at the clock. It was seven forty-five p.m. Robert had picked up Justin (the only son she would allow him to see) for his visitation at six o'clock. He was due to have him back by eight o'clock. *He better have him back by eight o'clock on the dot, or I'll call the police and have him arrested again*, she thought. *I have him right where I want him. He thinks he's better off without me. I'll show him better off. I'll have his ass arrested every time he looks at me the wrong way. I'll show him who he's dealing with.* She wanted him back. She longed for him. It was killing her that he had her served with divorce papers. Who knew what exactly was going on inside her alcoholic mind?

She was tormented. Somehow she thought that by bringing all of the charges against him, she would be able to bring him back in line. She had always been able to control him with threats. He had always come back to her. She wanted him. She needed him. All would be forgiven if he would come back to her and make this pain go away. If he didn't come back, she would make his life a living hell. Over her dead body would she allow him to see Teddy.

Teddy was her baby. Teddy loved her more than anyone else on this earth and she would protect her younger son at any cost. She wasn't even sure what she was protecting her son from. Things were muddled in her head. She had been drinking. It had been such a long time since she could think clearly. She called Robert on his cell phone. When he answered, she tried to sound sober. "Robert, it's Babette. When you bring Justin home, instead of just letting him off in front, please come in the front door and wait in the foyer. I have something I need to show you."

Robert Jacobs was confused. *What's she up to now?* he wondered. He did as she asked. He parked in front and walked into the house. Justin ran upstairs to see his brother. Babette appeared at the top of the stairs. She was wearing a see-thru negligee. He could see that underneath she was totally naked. *Has she lost her mind?* He didn't stop to ponder the situation. He turned around and walked out the door.

* * *

The next day, he told me what happened. I was astounded. "Look, Dr. Jacobs, you really don't need to tell me stuff like that. Actually, I don't want to *hear* stuff like that."

"I just want to show you, Lily, how Looney Tunes she really is. I don't want to take what she's offering, even for free."

Again I thought, *No one could make up this garbage.*

The whole day was spent on his problems. In between what was left of his patient caseload, he talked endlessly about his situation. He was not going to pay the mortgage.

"Where the hell does she think I'm getting the money for that? She refuses to pay anything at all, even though she's living upstairs in the house. She won't pay any of the utilities. She refuses to pay any bills whatsoever. She stole my patients; she raked me over the coals. I don't care if she's out on the street." I reminded him that he was still practicing dentistry in the basement of the house. "I don't care," he said. I asked him what his lawyer said about that. "You mean the great Mr. Batt? He doesn't care about anything except his fee." I pointed out to him, that by not paying the mortgage, his credit rating would be ruined. He didn't seem to care. It was another example of Dr. Jacobs thinking he was right, so things would have to turn out his way.

And so the great battle of the lawyers began. Her lawyer seemed to be quite a piranha, while his lawyer seemed to be quite docile. The e-mails flew back and forth. He constantly wanted me to read them, but I didn't want to do that. He insisted on reading some of them to me, anyway. It seemed that her lawyer was always throwing out accusations without answering any questions. His lawyer was always asking for information, which her lawyer would not give. These people were descending further and further into hell, and all the while, the financial and personal costs kept climbing.

Dr. Jacobs didn't have access to any of his personal stuff. There were weeks of legal entanglements. There was a restraining order against him. He could only get into his office at designated times. She had denied him any access to his younger child. He was facing criminal charges (as ridiculous as they were) for breaking his restraining order. I worried about the dentistry he was performing. He had lost all boundaries of professionalism. He told any patient who would listen all about the *bitch*.

Finally, his lawyer informed him that her lawyer said he could pick up his personal belongings at the back of the office (attached to the house) on a Friday night. "That's just great," he bellowed. "I'm not allowed in here from Friday night until Monday morning. How does she expect me to get my stuff?" I knew the next question before he asked it. "Lily, you have a key. Could you please go over to the office this weekend and get my things?"

I didn't want to do it, but I heard myself agree. "Ok, I'll put whatever I can fit into my car, and you can pick it up at my house."

What an adventure that turned out to be! I went to the house on Saturday morning and let myself in the office with my key. I could hear Dr. Tulip clomping around upstairs. I thought I would be quick. I would just get what I could fit into my car and then leave. There were about thirty trash bags in the back of the office. His clothes and personal things were stuffed inside. I didn't know where to begin. I got about four bags into my car and went back in to see what else I could get. Then I heard the "clump, clump, clump" on the stairs. I came face to face with Dr. Babette Tulip. She had a look of extreme hatred on her face. "Lily, this is my house! You get out of here right now, or I will call the police and have you charged with trespassing!" She was totally out of control. The office was in his name only. I was the office manager. I had every right to be there. I tried to look composed.

"Go ahead, call the police." I might have sounded brave, but I was shaking inside. I picked up two more bags and left.

"Why do you let yourself be put in that position?" Bill asked. "These people are totally crazy. You didn't have to pick up his clothes."

"I know," I said. I tried to explain. "I agree it sounds crazy. He really doesn't deserve my loyalty. I just somehow feel sorry for the guy. He is up against a real monster."

Later, Dr. Jacobs came to my house to pick up his things. "I'm sorry for putting you through that, Lily. I didn't think she would be home."

"It was pretty scary," I replied. "I do see what a completely irrational human being she can be."

Just then, Bill walked into the room. He walked over to Dr. Jacobs. "I have to tell you, Dr. Jacobs, that I don't appreciate having my wife put in that position."

Dr. Jacobs looked sheepish. "I know. I apologize to both of you." With that, Dr. Jacobs turned around and walked out of my house. Bill stood there, shaking his head. "Lily, you know this situation is not going to get any better."

"I know Bill. I'm sorry."

The situation only got worse. The only ones who seemed to benefit were the lawyers. The legal fees kept mounting. Dr. Jacobs kept complaining to anyone who would listen. He practically told anyone within earshot that he wished his wife were dead.

What he never told patients, however, was how he'd held a pair of scissors to his wife's throat. He told them that she was trumping up charges and had gotten a restraining order against him, and now she was using that restraining order to torture him. It was a half-truth. It was true she was using the incident to gain power over him, but I wasn't completely convinced he was remorseful enough over what he had done. This was a problem for me. I had never intended to be sympathetic to a wife abuser. I made sure that Dr. Jacobs knew my thoughts on the subject.

I brought it up again. "You know, Dr. Jacobs, I'm still having trouble with the fact that you threatened her with the scissors."

"Lily, I've explained that. She pushed me too far and I lost control. I hate myself for that. I went to anger management classes. I have lived every day since that incident with regret. You have to believe me."

"I know you regret it," I answered. "And I do agree that she is using the incident to her advantage. I just want to make it clear that I could never condone violence like that."

"Understood," he said.

No matter how I tried to convince him otherwise, he would not pay the mortgage. "The bitch is living here. I'm not living in the house. Let her pay."

"Was that legally settled? Did your lawyer tell you not to pay the mortgage?" I guess that was too logical a question for Dr. Jacobs.

"Listen, Lily, I'm not paying! Let the damn house go to foreclosure! Let the bitch get kicked out on her ass."

There was absolutely no reasoning with this man. Never mind that his practice was in the house. Never mind that his kids were living in the house. He was paying a fortune in legal fees. He was convinced he was right. In his mind, Babette had "thrown him under the bus," and he wasn't going to give her one dime. "She's a dentist. She can pay her own damned bills," he countered.

Vicious does not begin to describe what was going on. He told me to disconnect the Internet every night. She was supposedly not allowed into the office, just as he was not allowed into the house. He said he was not going to allow her to mooch off of the Internet that he was paying for. This went on for a couple of weeks. I got to work one morning to find out that the whole system had been taken out of the office. Apparently, she had hired a technician to disconnect everything and move it upstairs.

He was livid. We had to get a whole new system put in.

Dr. Jacobs was frequently gone from the office. He had legal appointments, psychologist appointments, and meetings with the custody evaluators. And on top of it all, Dr. Tulip filed a complaint with the dental board relating to how he supposedly "barged into her office" on the day he was served with the restraining order.

The battle seemed to be never ending. In my wildest dreams, I never could have imagined how anyone's divorce could be quite this ugly. She was out to destroy him. All he could think and talk about was what she was doing to him and how evil she was. The worst part was the way she kept the younger son away from him. It seemed that, because of the restraining order against him, he couldn't get any leverage to fight for his custody—or even visitation rights.

It was getting almost impossible to have a normal conversation with him. He was getting letters from the bank. The house was definitely headed for foreclosure. "You can't just let the house go to foreclosure," I said, trying again to talk some sense into him.

"I don't care, Lily. She refuses to pay anything. That bozo lawyer of hers keeps saying I need to pay the entire thing. They can go screw themselves. I don't have the money to pay the mortgage. I'm now so far behind, it's impossible."

The only impossible thing, I thought, *is him.* Who was he kidding? What kind of nut case was he? Did he really think he could just stop paying the mortgage and somehow everything would turn out in his favor?

What was actually going on made little difference in Dr. Jacobs' mind. He totally believed himself to be the victim. Babette had bullied him for years. He had put up with her alcoholism. She refused to admit she even had a drinking problem. He was convinced the scissors incident had happened because she drove him over the edge. She used it to get a restraining order against him. Then she brought false charges against him for breaking that restraining order. She stole most of his patients. She wouldn't let him see his youngest child. She had made his life a living hell. He was *not* going to pay for the mortgage. "Let them evict the bitch!"

He hated her for all she had done. Hell, she was still doing it. He had a plan. He was going to leave that office way before the bank foreclosed on the house (where the office was downstairs.) He was already pre-approved for a business loan to relocate to a new office. The approval had come through several months before. He was just waiting to get a lease on a good location. Once he moved the practice out of that house, she could just go to hell.

"Aren't you worried your credit will be ruined before you ever get to move the office?" I once again asked this question of him one afternoon.

"Lily, stop it! I know what I'm doing. It was a business loan. The money is waiting for me. I just have to work out the details of the lease for the new office I'm eyeing." This was so typical of Dr. Jacobs. Because he thought he was right, he actually believed things would happen the way he wanted them to. I couldn't figure out why he kept thinking that way. Things were definitely not working out his way. He was playing a dangerous game. He was risking his credit rating. I didn't know how he expected this new office thing to work out when he hadn't paid the mortgage on the house for months.

We didn't have to wait long to see what would happen. The mortgage company sent him a notice of impending foreclosure. They were giving him a grace period. They would make every attempt to work with him, but if he could not pay, he would get another letter, sometime in the next thirty days. He then would have an additional thirty days before the bank took possession of the house. He was still playing chicken with the house. "She has to pay her share, or she'll be out on her ass," he said, in reference to the bank's warnings. Then, as if things were not bad enough, the bank cancelled his business loan. He lost the money he had been counting on to lease and to remodel another office. Of course, Dr. Jacobs did not own up to his responsibility for losing the loan.

"What are you going to do?" I asked.

"Lily, short of killing myself, I don't know what to do. I have to get out of this office. Maybe I can rent space in another office somewhere. I don't know anything, except that bitch has ruined my life."

The office had become a dismal, toxic place. I was still there, but I was starting to be disappointed in myself for continuing to stick it out. Even though Dr. Jacobs was mostly the cause of his own misery, I did feel sorry for him. He was in a mess. I tried to organize my thoughts by writing it down.

Dr. Jacobs let his wife dominate him for all those years.

The way he fought back was to scream, yell, and have tantrums.

She was an alcoholic and totally irrational.

She wanted to totally control him.

She had relentlessly nagged and belittled him for years.

He was not mature enough to walk away when he could.

He lost it, and he did abuse her with the scissors threat.

She relished blackmailing him.

Once she got the restraining order, she used it to add on all kinds of fake charges.

She was actually obsessed with him. She wanted to own him. She was never going to let him go.

She was using their younger son to get to him.

He did not have a clue how to get himself out of this mess.

Writing this list helped me understand how the situation had gotten to this point. I had to admit that Dr. Jacobs was an immature jerk, but somehow, I still felt sorry for him.

I could not imagine how all of this would eventually end.

I wanted Bill to understand. That was one of the reasons I had to put the list down on paper. I showed it to Bill. His comment was, "Lily, you're only fooling yourself if you think there will be a good ending to this."

* * *

RAUNCHY RENDEZVOUS

Chapter 23

D r. Tulip lay naked on the top of her bed. She was watching her lover, Donald, get dressed. *He'll do,* she thought. *At least he satisfies me. I have needs.* Robert doesn't give a damn. She had been drinking before Donald came over. First, she called Robert while she was drunk. Robert hung up on her. Then she called Donald. He was always ready to come over when she needed him. Donald was Dr. Donald Depore, the dentist for whom she had once done part-time work. When she and Robert were originally separated, and even after they got back together, she did part-time work—sometimes as a dentist, but usually as a hygienist. She worked a couple of days a week at Donald Depore's office. She could tell he had a roving eye, then, but she didn't take the bait at that time. She had just gotten back with Robert and she didn't want to spoil it. But now, things were different. Robert was being a prick. She had every right to do whatever she wanted to do. Donald had great hands—hands that could readily satisfy her. She and Donald became reacquainted when, by coincidence, they showed up at the same dental seminar. The last time he laid eyes on her, she was back with her husband. He asked her about that. She told him she was now separated again, and this time it would stay that way. They talked to each other at great length that day. She gave him the impression he could call her. She knew he was married. Of course, she had worked for him and his wife, Sara. She didn't care. She was entitled to live life as she pleased.

Their affair began soon after their chance meeting. They made love as often as they could. Donald said he and his wife didn't get along. He said his wife was frigid and no longer desired sex. He claimed he stayed with her for the sake of their children. Who cared, anyway? Donald made her feel alive. Robert didn't want her anymore. The only problem was that, when Donald touched her, she thought of Robert. Robert was the one she really wanted. It didn't look as though Robert was coming back to her. None of her threats had worked. Filing that restraining order hadn't worked the way she had hoped. Nothing seemed to be working out the way she had planned. She wanted Robert on his knees. She wanted him to beg her forgiveness. She needed a drink. Gin always made it better. Gin made everything better.

Donald was very successful. He actually had two offices. One office was in Livingston, the other in Verona. The office in Livingston was especially plush. Money—he had lots of money. As Babette Tulip watched Donald get dressed, she began thinking about the money. Why wasn't she married to someone who could give her all the things she deserved in life? Maybe, when the time was right, she could somehow have access to some of Donald's money. She didn't know how, yet. She was tired. Donald was leaving. She would go to sleep and think about it in the morning.

Donald Depore got home and took a shower. He needed to wash off the smell of Babette's too-sweet perfume, mixed with the smell of her liquor. He didn't think his wife suspected anything. He slipped into bed beside his sleeping wife. He really did love her. He just needed a diversion. He had always needed diversions. None of these liaisons ever lasted very long. Over the years, if his wife Sara ever suspected anything she never showed it. He made a good living—enough to give Sara a lavish lifestyle. So what, if he needed a release now and then? He could still satisfy Sara sexually—just not on the same night he would see Babette. Sara awakened. "You're home late from the meeting. How was it?"

"It was the usual boring stuff," he replied. "Go to bed sweetheart." Sara was up now. She swept her hand over her husband's body. He caught her hand. "I'm really tired, maybe tomorrow." He turned on his side and went to sleep. Sara stayed awake for a long while. She thought about what she had been actively avoiding thinking about for a very long time.

Just a few blocks away, Robert Jacobs was tossing and turning. Sleep would not come. His mind was wide-awake. The bitch had tried to call him earlier that evening. She was drunk. It seemed as if she were always drunk. How was he ever going to get out of this mess? She was the most vengeful woman he ever had the misfortune to know. She had ruined him. He was facing foreclosure and the bank had revoked his loan to start a new business. Where was he going to practice? What was he going to do? He finally fell asleep wishing that Dr. Babette Tulip would just vanish from the face of the earth.

* * *

Chapter 24

Sara Depore hesitated in front of the door. The sign read: MICHAEL LISTER, PRIVATE INVESTIGA-TOR. He had come highly recommended by one of Sara's neighbors, who had used Mr. Lister to get the goods on her own husband. Sara took a deep breath and went in. If Sara had not trusted this particular neighbor as much as she did, she would have turned around and left. The office, although in a decent part of town, was quite shabby. The waiting room furniture was very old and heavily worn. The walls were in sorry need of a good paint job. It was odd, but with everything on Sara's mind, the thought went through her head that live plants would really help the place. There was a reception desk, but there was no receptionist to be found. The door slammed behind Sara. Then Michael Lister appeared from an adjoining room. "Mrs. Depore, I'm Michael Lister."

"Yes, Mr. Lister, I spoke with you on the phone. My neighbor highly recommended you."

"Come in, Mrs. Depore. Tell me what brings you here."

Michael Lister listened intently to what Sara Depore had to say. It was an old story—cheating husband, suspicious wife. He had done many cases like this in his four years as a "Private Dick." In his wildest dreams, he never thought he would find himself in this profession. But, as they say, "necessity is the mother of invention," and Michael had been forced to reinvent himself after that messy affair with the bank. He had been a trusted employee there for fifteen years. That was, until he embezzled twenty thousand dollars from them.

He was caught. He pleaded guilty and had thrown himself on the mercy of the court. He had needed the money for his teeth. Those hacks, Dr. Jacobs and his bimbo wife, Dr. Tulip, together had ruined his mouth. He needed the money to go to a *real* dentist and fix the damage. Dr. Barry Rosenstein was the top rated dentist in the area. Michael wanted to be sure about who was doing the work this time. Dr. Rosenstein did a beautiful job. At the time, Michael saw no other way out. The court was lenient with him. He was sentenced to five years, but only ended up having to serve one. It was hard to find a job after that. An old buddy of his hired him as an assistant for his failing private detective agency. As it turned out, Michael actually had a flair for this type of work. When his buddy died of a sudden heart attack six months later, Michael took over the business. He was actually making a reasonable living from it.

Now he was listening to every word Sara Depore told him. He would take the case. They agreed on the amount. Michael could tell this woman was well fixed. He would do a good job for her. He would start right away. If she were satisfied, maybe he could pick up a couple more accounts of this caliber.

* * *

I was in the office early that morning. I wondered what time Dr. Jacobs would decide to show up. He was hardly ever on time, anymore. He always had an excuse. This day was no different. The first patient had already been waiting fifteen minutes when Dr. Jacobs arrived. As soon as he came through the door, he motioned for me to come to the back of the office. I was always uncomfortable when that happened, and it happened a lot. Although the patient had been waiting and the doctor was already fifteen minutes late, he wanted to waste even more time by having me come to the back to undoubtedly hear his problems—again.

"The bitch called me last night. She was drunk as usual. I don't know how much more of this I can take. I already owe fifty grand to my lawyer, and it's not getting any better. She's got me over a barrel with these charges of hers. There's no end in sight." He sighed deeply. "The house is headed for foreclosure. I don't know where or how to relocate the practice. Things are a fucking mess." As usual, I didn't know quite what to do except stand there. He had nothing new to tell me.

"Dr. Jacobs," I said, "your patient is waiting."

The rest of the day was stressful. We had more cancellations. Not only was that further indication the practice was going down the tubes, but it also gave Dr. Jacobs more time to hang around my desk and complain. It was becoming a distasteful chore to remain in that office. I didn't know how much more of this rancid atmosphere I could endure. What used to be somewhat interesting had become truly unbearable.

I wondered why all of the patients didn't just quit the practice. I didn't know what they were thinking when

Dr. Jacobs would leave the operatory several times while treating them. Each time he would leave the patient in the chair, he would say, "Hold on, I will be right back." Then he would check his messages on his cell phone, or worse, come to my desk to continue telling me what a horrible drunken wench his wife was.

I didn't know how all of this would end. My dread increased. I started to formulate a plan for leaving. I could not picture myself working in this polluted atmosphere forever. Bill had been telling me to get out of there. I now believed he was right. Somehow, I had a weird attachment to Dr. Jacobs. I definitely felt sorry for him. I didn't think he had been treated fairly. Things were really closing in on him, now. I knew he had brought a lot of this on himself. His controlling behavior, his temper, and his immaturity all had played a part. Yet, he had been no match for her. Dr. Babette Tulip; she was a manipulative human being beyond all imagination. I definitely believed all of the things he told me about her. I had witnessed enough of her behavior to make his claims credible. I wished I could help him, but I knew that sticking around was not going to solve the problem. I didn't know how I was going to tell him. I would have to give him notice, of course, but I wasn't sure how or when I would do it. He had grown dependent on me. I didn't want to add to his troubles, but I knew this situation had grown unhealthy for me. I thought about it all of the time. It wasn't my life. Why should I be so involved? I decided to talk to Bill that night. I had made a decision to quit. I would tell Dr. Jacobs in the morning. How could I have known that fate had other plans?

* * *

Chapter 25

Babette Tulip could not sleep. She didn't know how she was going to pay her bills. Her new practice was not doing very well. She wasn't taking in as many new patients as she had hoped. Nothing in her life was going very well. Robert was probably lost to her forever. None of her ploys had brought him back to her. He was not paying her bills. The lawyers were still fighting over who would pay what, but nothing was settled. Her credit cards were maxed out. She still needed to pay on the loan for her new office. Robert was not paying the mortgage on the house, where she was still living upstairs from his dental office. Everything was a mess. When she filed the restraining order, she had meant to just teach him a lesson. She was sure he would have come back to her by now. Instead, he filed for divorce, and things just went downhill from there. Nothing was going her way. Donald was a diversion—and a rich one at that. Why shouldn't he help her? She would make him help her.

She braced herself with her usual fix of gin and scotch. Then she called Donald on his cell. She was not supposed to do that. He picked up. "Babette, what are you doing?

Sara is asleep, but she could have heard my cell ringing. You're not supposed to call me when I could be at home."

"I know Donald," she cooed seductively, "but I really need to see you. *please!*"

She went down the hall and checked on her sleeping sons. They were sound sleepers and were down for the night. She took a hot shower and put on her most seductive negligee. She waited for Donald to come, as she knew he would.

When she heard his car in the driveway, she ran downstairs to open the door for him. A few minutes later, they were making love. She wanted to make tonight her best-ever performance. She remembered to do everything she knew Donald liked. She needed to make him want her and be willing to do anything for her.

When they were both spent, she curled up under his arm. "How was it sweetie?" She whispered. "No one can give you what I can. You know I'm right. I know you do."

"Yeah, baby, you're good all right. No doubt about that."

She wanted more from him. "Tell me how good, Donald. Tell me you can't live without me."

He lifted himself up on one elbow. What exactly was she getting at? He looked at her. He stared at her naked breasts. He ran his fingers through her red hair, spread across the pillow. "Listen, Babette, you know I like being with you. But I don't know exactly what you're getting at."

She jumped out of the bed. "What am I getting at?" she confronted him. "I want more Donald! I need more!"

At that point, he too got out of bed. "Babette, we talked about this. I can't leave Sara. I *won't* leave Sara."

She was getting really angry. "That mousy woman— she can't give you what I can give you, Donald."

He was getting very nervous at this point. He crossed over to where she was standing and took hold of her arms. They were both naked, and they were both emotionally charged.

"All right, Donald," she said, "stay with your wonderful wife, but it will cost you."

"What exactly does that mean?" he asked, digging his fingers deeper into her arms.

"What do you think it means?" she asked. "I need money, Donald. I need lots of money. You need to take care of me, or I just may need to pay a visit to your precious little Sara."

"Who the hell do you think you are?" he exploded. He tightened his grip on her arms and violently shook her. Startled, she tried to take a step back from him, but his grip was too strong. They struggled. Somehow, as he was shaking her, he pushed her. She fell backward into the lamp. In seconds, she lay sprawled on the floor, naked, with blood gushing from her head.

He stared at her for a second. Panic engulfed him. Later, he couldn't remember how he hurriedly got into his clothes and drove away. He felt like he was suffocating. He needed to run. Somehow, he got himself home and into the safety of his wife's bed.

Michael Lister had been parked outside the entire time. He had begun his new assignment, following Donald Depore, just that evening. He saw Donald enter the house, and about an hour later, Michael saw him run out of there, as if he were being chased by fire. He thought that was strange. He was surprised where Donald had gone that night. It was the house where Dr. Robert Jacobs and Dr. Babette Tulip had practiced together. It was the house where, in the basement dental office, they had ruined his teeth and ruined his life. He had heard that the two dentists were separated. At the time, when he heard about the separation, he certainly did not care. Life could be strange. At that moment, he had no idea just how strange. He was pleased he would have something to report to Sara Depore.

Michael went home that night and tried to piece things together in his head. He had struck pay dirt. It looked like Dr. Donald Depore was having an affair with Dr. Babette Tulip. He didn't know quite why Dr. Depore had looked so desperate when he ran out of the house. He would have to do some more investigating. Either way, he was proud of himself. On his first evening on his new assignment, he had been extremely successful. Maybe his reputation would grow. Maybe he could make a good living out of this "private dick" stuff.

* * *

Chapter 26

I talked to Bill when I got home that night. "I've had it with that crazy office," I declared.

"You know what, Lily?" Bill replied. "Enough is enough already. Just quit!"

"Done!" I responded. This time I meant it. In the morning, I would give Dr. Jacobs my two weeks notice. I slept well that night. I had finally made a monumental decision—one that was quite overdue.

The doorbell rang very early the next morning. I was anxious to get to work because this was the day I planned to deliver my two weeks notice. When I opened the door, there were two men flashing badges, and they asked if they could come in. What I heard next was one of the biggest shocks of my life.

Two detectives sat in my living room. When they told me what had happened, I felt like I was outside of my body. I felt as though I were observing the police, as they talked to someone else. I felt confused. I didn't know if I could be sure what I heard was really being said.

It seemed that Dr. Tulip had been found in a near-dead condition early that same morning. Maria, her housekeeper, always arrived at the house before six o'clock. It was her custom, after letting herself in with her key, to make coffee and then take it into Dr. Tulip's room. Dr. Tulip usually needed a couple of cups before she could even get out of bed. Maria knew Dr. Tulip was usually hung over. It wasn't her job to say anything about it. After waking up Dr. Tulip and taking the coffee to her, Maria would then make breakfast, wake up the boys, and get them ready for school. This morning, when she went into Dr. Tulip's bedroom, she found Dr. Tulip sprawled out on the floor, naked, and covered in blood. Her initial impulse was to scream, but she thought of the boys. She loved those boys. She had taken care of them since they were born. She needed to regain her composure. She called 911, and then she woke up the boys and quickly got them out of the house and over to a neighbor's. She told them just to trust her, and they did whatever she told them to do.

Police and rescue arrived within minutes. Dr. Tulip was taken to the hospital. Her condition was critical. She had lost a lot of blood. The police interrogated Maria. She gave them all of the information she could. She told them how Dr. Jacobs had been threatening Dr. Tulip. The neighbor, who was also a patient of Dr. Jacobs, gave them the name of the front desk person who worked in the office. She knew me because we had talked extensively whenever she had an appointment.

The police were interrogating anyone they could think of who might know something about the case. They suspected foul play. They didn't think Dr. Tulip had just fallen into the lamp. They theorized she had been pushed. They thought it was an attempted murder. I told them how shocked I was to hear all of this. They requested I go to the police station with them, so they could officially take down any information I could give them.

The police interrogation was grueling. I cringed when they asked me about the relationship between Dr. Tulip and her husband. I told them the truth, but I tried not to go into too much detail. Then they asked me if Dr. Jacobs had ever threatened Dr. Tulip. I was scared. I did not want to incriminate Dr. Jacobs, but I couldn't lie for him, either. When they asked me, I had to tell them what I knew. Apparently, they had already heard from other sources how Dr. Jacobs often said he wished his wife were dead. They asked me if I ever heard him say those words. I told them I had, but I believed these to be just empty threats, and he never would have acted on them. I tried to tell them Dr. Jacobs was just all talk, and he would never hurt anyone, but my pleas were to no avail.

A lot of people had witnessed Dr. Jacobs utter these threats. He had told many people—patients, colleagues, and the guys at the cigar shop. They all, at one time or another, had heard him say he wanted her dead. Very soon, a warrant was issued for his arrest.

While Dr. Jacobs was being arrested, Dr. Tulip was clinging to life. It seemed she had suffered a brain injury. The tests all showed she had brain activity, but she was not waking up. The doctors were not sure how long it would be before she would gain consciousness. She had lost a lot of blood, and she was given multiple transfusions. Maria had called Dr. Tulip's mother, and the boys were safely with their grandmother.

My head was swimming. I tried to get a grip on what had happened. The house and the office below it where I had worked were decked out in yellow crime-scene police tape. Dr. Jacobs was in jail, and Dr. Tulip was in critical condition. Had he tried to kill her? I knew he wanted her dead. I knew he had made threats all over town. Yet, somehow, I didn't believe he had tried to kill her.

I felt sick to my stomach. How could all of this have happened? Was there something I could have done to prevent this? Why hadn't I listened to Bill? I had known for a long time this situation was dangerous. I was way over my head when I tried to talk sense into Dr. Jacobs. Thoughts went flying in and out of my head. Could it be possible? Could he have done such a thing? I always came back to the conclusion that he couldn't have. But I still kept wondering. If he had not done it, then who had?

* * *

Michael Lister learned about the attempt on Dr. Tulip's life on the evening news. He sat glued to his TV set, trying to make sense of what he had just heard. "Dr. Robert Z. Jacobs was in jail for the attempted murder of his estranged wife, Dr. Babette Tulip." *Wow*! Michael had been parked outside the house the whole time it was happening. He saw Dr. Donald Depore flee the scene. He needed to process what he had seen. He had despised those two dentists for a long time. They hadn't just ruined his teeth several years before, they had ruined his life, as well. He thought of how he had embezzled money from the bank where he had once worked and how he had served time for his crime. He thought how he had lost a job he loved and could never again be hired in the financial business. He thought about how the only job he could find was as a private detective. He had struggled to even get that job—because of his prison record. "Damn them! Damn them both," he said out loud. "He can just rot in jail for what he's done to me." Then he decided that, in a few days, he would call Sara Depore and tell her that, after following her husband for a while, he could find nothing. He would tell her he was giving up the case.

* * *

DEVASTATION AND CONFUSION

Chapter 27

D r. Jacobs had lost everything. Bail was denied. The court decided he was a flight risk. He was out of money. He completely went through what little assets he had left. He had already paid everything to the lawyer who handled his divorce. The house was in foreclosure. His practice was gone. He was forced to use a court-appointed public defender. He could not afford to pay for a private criminal lawyer. He was on suicide watch. The man was completely devastated. *How did it come to this?* he wondered. Alone in his cell, he asked himself that question over and over again. Yes, he hated her. Yes, he wished her dead. But try to kill her? Never!

Everything important to him was gone. His boys were with Babette's mother. That hurt most of all. He might never see them again. He wondered how Babette was doing. He knew she was in critical condition. He knew she had a brain injury. He actually wanted her to recover. She could tell the police it wasn't him who tried to kill her. Then he wondered if she would really vindicate him if she could, or would she be just as happy to have him languish in prison?

* * *

The police let me into the office to clear up loose ends. I needed to call the patients. Almost all of them knew about the tragedy. Either they had seen it on the news or read about it in the papers. If patients knew where they wanted copies of their records sent, I obliged them. Otherwise, I just packed the records in boxes and turned them over to the police. I felt sad, angry, bewildered, and worried. I felt horrible for Dr. Jacobs. I didn't want to believe he had tried to kill his wife, but deep in my gut, I couldn't be certain. I even felt sorry for Dr. Tulip. I didn't know what was going to happen. Bill said I needed a break. He said I should just take some time and not even attempt to look for another job right away. He said I could even think about retiring indefinitely. I was grateful for that, and I rapidly agreed to not even think about working for the time being. I needed to recover from this whole catastrophe.

The police interviewed everyone they thought would have some knowledge of the relationship between Dr. Jacobs and Dr. Tulip. Dr. Jacobs had run his mouth to many patients. He often told them how much he hated his wife. Ramona Green, Dr. Tulip's front-desk manager, was quick to say Dr. Tulip was afraid of Dr. Jacobs. The men at the cigar shop all agreed that Dr. Jacobs constantly said he wished his wife were dead. The prosecuting attorney was carefully building his case. The DNA evidence on the sheets from the attempted murder scene did not match that of Dr. Jacobs. However, the prosecuting attorney was sure Dr. Jacobs was guilty, and he was hell-bent on proving it. He hated wife-abusers. He had seen his share in his day, and he was not going to let this one get away.

* * *

Meanwhile, at the hospital, Dr. Babette Tulip was going through her own private hell.

She could hear. She could only make out noises, at first. They were extremely faint in the beginning. Then they became louder. At first, she didn't know what the words meant. She knew she was hearing words in a language she found familiar, but she couldn't quite make out their meaning. There were sounds all around her. There was some kind of buzzing or humming going on. Maybe it was the sound of machines—or some kind of equipment. It was hard to differentiate between the sounds of language and the sounds of the machines. She was frightened. She didn't know where she was or what was happening all around her.

Days passed. She still had no idea where she was. The confusion was devastating. The outside voices and noises continued. She needed to wake up. If only she could wake up. Was she dreaming? Was she dead? She didn't think so. *Please*, she screamed in her head, *please, someone help me.*

The doctors were baffled. Why was Babette Tulip not coming out of this comatose state? By all accounts, she should be waking up. All of the tests showed brain activity. Her wounds were healing. They feared that the longer she remained unconscious, the greater the danger of permanent damage. Time would tell.

* * *

The newspapers were having a field day. The headlines screamed, "Dentist accused of attempted murder of his estranged wife." The story always included details about the alleged abuse and the restraining order. To my horror and mortification, I was also mentioned. "Lily Morgan, Office Manager, often heard Dr. Jacobs say he wished his wife were dead." This was not at all what I intended. I had told the truth—all of it. I had made it clear I believed these were just idle threats. But the newspapers wanted to sensationalize everything, and that's exactly what they did. I became more and more depressed over the situation. Bill was wonderful to me. He never said, "I told you so."

Several weeks passed. Dr. Jacobs was in jail awaiting trial for the attempted murder of his wife. Dr. Tulip was still comatose. I was still traumatized by all of the events of the past weeks. I stayed awake at night, wondering. Was there something I could have done? I didn't want to leave my house. I had never felt like this before. I had been stunned beyond belief. Could I have seen this coming? Maybe so. I really didn't know. I played everything over and over again in my mind. Why had I stayed at that office so long? I knew these people were crazy. I knew the situation was dangerous. Or did I? Did I turn a blind eye? I didn't know. The questions were making me more and more depressed. Bill was wonderful. He said I was too hard on myself, and time would clear things up. Still, I constantly caught myself wondering whether or not

Dr. Jacobs actually committed the crime. I didn't think he was capable of it. But then again, the question kept popping up inside my head. "Who *did* try to kill Dr. Tulip, if not Dr. Jacobs?"

* * *

Meanwhile, Michael Lister was tormented. As planned, he waited a few days and then told Sara Depore he had been following her husband for several days, and nothing had come of it. He told Sara he thought her husband was clean, and she should just save her money. Sara was anxious to believe her husband was faithful, so she accepted what Michael told her.

Michael was anxious. He still wanted Dr. Jacobs to rot in jail. He wanted to see him convicted. In Michael's mind, Dr. Jacobs didn't try to kill his wife, but he had killed Michael's life. That hack dentist had taken everything from him, and it was payback time. But Michael Lister had, at one time, been an upstanding citizen. He still had a conscience. It was that damned conscience that kept telling him to tell the truth. He tried to silence his conscience every time it spoke to him. Adding to the turmoil was fear. He was afraid that, sooner or later, the truth would come out and he would be arrested for withholding evidence. He couldn't go to prison again. He had been lucky last time. He had been given a light sentence. He couldn't imagine what would happen this time if he were arrested and convicted. He thought a lot about the downward spiral of events that had brought him to this point. It had all started with his teeth. Those hack dentists had ruined his teeth.

Michael was wrestling with all these thoughts, as he was driving home from his office. He was deep in thought. He didn't know what he was going to do. He didn't realize he had veered too far to the right. He didn't see the tree on the side of the road until it was too late. He hit the tree head-on.

Chapter 28

Michael was in extremely serious condition. He had suffered massive injuries. Several organs had been damaged, and he required surgery. His prognosis was uncertain. He was kept constantly sedated.

In the same hospital, one floor down, Babette Tulip remained in her coma. She constantly screamed inside her head. Day in and day out she was locked inside of herself. *Why can't I speak? Why can't they hear me screaming? Please, someone, please help me!* She was terrified. There were strange noises everywhere. She didn't know where she was. She didn't know if it were day or night. Could she be sure she was even alive? Could this be hell?

Dr. Jacobs was on a continuous suicide watch. The prison psychiatrist said he was a definite risk. The court-appointed criminal lawyer, who was defending him, tried to give him some hope. He reminded Dr. Jacobs that someone else's DNA had been found on the sheets that night. The prosecution really did not have definite evidence to tie him to the crime, except, of course that Dr. Jacobs had let it be known all over town how he wanted his wife dead.

In addition, he did not have an alibi for that night. Also, Dr. Jacobs had a history of violence. The scissors incident and the restraining order were a matter of record. The trial date was coming up. The defense was not very strong.

* * *

A couple of months passed. I was doing a little better. At Bill's encouragement, I saw a psychologist. It helped. Marcie was there for me. So was Kimmie, but she had graduated from college and taken a job out of state. Kimmie had really grown up. We talked every day. We were still very close, but she was no longer so dependent on me. I still blamed myself for a lot of things, but I was beginning to ease up on the guilt. My only crime was staying in that crazy office way too long. I did wonder about Dr. Jacobs and how he was doing. I read in the local newspaper that his trial was coming up very soon. I still did not know whether or not he was guilty. I knew it was possible, but in my heart, I did not want to believe it.

* * *

There was a flurry of activity going on in Michael Lister's room. He was awake and feeling better. He told the nurse he needed to talk to the police—NOW!

* * *

IT'S OVER

Chapter 29

"How do I look, Mom?" Kimmie asked. She was about to be married. She was the most beautiful bride I had ever seen. I was not just happy, I was joyous. Kimmie, my beautiful daughter, was marrying a wonderful man. Bill and I were about to walk her down the aisle. Had it been just two years ago when I was deeply depressed over a situation that had engulfed my every thought? All of that was behind me now. Things had worked out the way they were supposed to.

Michael Lister had told the police about Donald Depore, and Dr. Depore was arrested. His DNA matched the DNA found on Dr. Tulip's sheets that fateful night. Dr. Depore confessed, and charges were dropped against Dr. Jacobs.

I did see Dr. Jacobs one more time. I had put the whole incident behind me when I got a call from him. He was renting space in a small office in a rather depressing apartment building in East Orange. It was all he could afford. He said he had been thinking about me and would love to see me. At first, I declined, but then I decided to go.

I was shocked at what I saw. The office was truly a dump. I felt very sad for him. He had been forced to declare bankruptcy. He needed to start from scratch. This was all he could afford to rent. He was slowly, very slowly, building up a new patient base. The patients who came to this office were more likely to choose extractions, rather than have to pay for restorative work. But it was a start.

I asked about his boys. He had them! He actually had them! Once he agreed to extensive counseling, the courts let him have his sons. He could finally admit his own part in the total disaster. He could now understand how his temper had been out of control, and he could actually see his own responsibility in the devastating course of events, which followed. Babette Tulip continued to be comatose, going on more than two years, now. The doctors were still baffled. No one could even guess what her eventual outcome would be.

We chatted for a while, Dr. Jacobs and I. "You know, Lily, if you ever want a job with me, you've got it." I was somewhat taken aback. "No thank you, Dr. Jacobs, I think I will just pass."

I have heard on several occasions that whatever one puts out into the universe—that is what one can expect back. I don't know if it is true or not. We all know life is not always fair. I do believe, however, the hate generating from that dental office in West Orange, New Jersey, was powerful and destructive. Hate is what Dr. Tulip put out there, and hate is what came back to her. Dr. Jacobs put out hate and uncontrolled rage, and he certainly paid the price. Those two dentists truly caused themselves to disintegrate in every way possible. Their mental breakdowns were devastating. They truly had "Gone Dental."

My thoughts were interrupted, as the music started, and Bill and I proudly escorted Kimmie down the aisle.